Iva Be

Veronica's Bookstore

Veronica's Bookstore © 2021 Iva Beranek
Publisher: Independent Publishing Network

Author: Iva Beranek
Email: iva.ana.beranek@gmail.com
You can contact Iva and follow her on Instagram @ivadublin.

All rights reserved. No part of this book may be reproduced in any form or by any electronic or mechanical means, including information storage and retrieval systems, without permission in writing from the publisher, except by reviewers, who may quote brief passages in a review.

Mary Kathleen Glavich, SND, editor
Illustrations by Tatiana Andreieva
Graphics design by Momir Blažek

ISBN: 978-1-80049-912-6

British Library Cataloguing in Publication Data.
A catalogue record for this book is available from the British Library.

I dedicate the book
to Erik and Tara,
my nephew and niece

Acknowledgments

When I was a child, before I knew how to read and write, I got used to listening to bedtime stories at home. Later on, my parents taught me to write, and bought me books, which inspired my love of reading. I am grateful for the education which I was given and for the teachers that I had. As a child I loved to play with toys as well as with friends, which nurtured my imagination. I am grateful to my parents who allowed me to immerse myself in play growing up. I am grateful for the love that my family gave to me, as well as for the encouragement to develop my skills, and follow my dreams.

My great aunt Ana influenced me a lot. She was a master storyteller, who knew how to foster innocence in children. She spoke to me about God and it is because of her I believe that I am a Christian. Even though she died when I was quite young, I still remember her with fondness, and perhaps without her influence this book wouldn't ever have been written.

I am grateful for the many friends who cheered me on through the various stages of writing and publishing. I am grateful to Fr. Bill Toner SJ who read the first draft of the book and helped me to polish it a little by offering his wise and helpful comments. I am grateful to have worked with Mary Kathleen Glavich, SND, a very skilled editor. It was a joy to work with her and I am immensely grateful for her insights and the time that she took in editing my book. I have also worked with Tatiana Andreieva, a very talented illustrator, who was very patient with my requests. She did such a fantastic job on the illustrations. I am truly grateful to Momir Blažek, a graphic designer and a friend, who put the manuscript into the book format. Ivana Han and Karen Rodriguez gave such beautiful endorsements of the book - thank you both!

As a Catholic, I am grateful for knowing Christians of other denominations, because their friendship and ecumenical cooperation offered me a wider experience of Christian faith. Life is much more beautiful when we embrace each other as brothers and sisters in Christ.

Above all, I am grateful to Jennifer for being my greatest cheer-leader. I am also grateful to Silvia and Nora, who as loyal friends always affirmed my writing and told me to get it out there. I am grateful to Martin for believing in me and for giving me constructive feedback in the process of publishing this book. I am grateful to Marie for her fantastic support as a friend, as well as for helping me with my English. Naturally, some of my gratitude cannot simply be put into words, yet I hope that those who supported me on this journey know how much I appreciated it.

Lastly, and most of all I am grateful to God. I am grateful to Jesus for all the lessons in life, for guiding me, inspiring me, loving me and allowing me to share some of the treasures of my heart with others. Jesus also loved telling stories. I hope that something of His love will overflow through the pages of this book, and inspire the reader to not ever give up.

Iva Beranek

Endorsements

"In her book *Veronica's Bookstore*, Iva intertwines echoes from a long forgotten past with the present wondrous world of Matthew Alden, age eight. As the precocious boy uncovers the storied life of his grandmother, a tale of imploring secrets unfolds, and weaves itself into lessons on innocence and hope. This book is a gift that will inspire any child to cherish family and friendship!"
— **Karen Rodriguez**, creator of *The Grace Lane Chronicles*

"*Veronica's bookstore* is one of those books that you don't want to put down until you finish reading it. The story moves slowly and gently, and that's how it draws you into the plot, with a constant sense of excitement about what will happen next.

The story revolves around the boy Matthew and his family, especially his grandmother who is deceased but still present, through the dreams and deeds she left as her legacy. I cannot fail to notice the theme of faith that extends throughout the book even in the relationship of the deceased grandmother and grandchild. We are reminded of the communion of saints; we on Earth are connected with the faithful in Heaven in spiritual unity. A sense of magic is present here, which would instantly attract my boys.

I loved it too, but what is more Iva has a wonderful way of intertwining true values with the story. She bravely spoke about the topics of discrimination that are current, yet it was done in a dignified, instructive way that children can understand.

I was especially won over by the late grandmother's advice on how to preserve a child's innocence. This is something we forget growing up. Interesting how this came from the pen of an adult woman, who obviously still sees the world through childlike eyes, a virtue we all too often neglect.

The book contains so much wisdom and has strong messages. Here is one of my favourites: "... *to keep your childhood innocence laugh a lot... And how do you learn a joyful attitude? By practicing it. It's not only in laughter that joy is expressed, it also comes out through thoughts and actions"*.

In this book every child would get the inspiration to build self-esteem and will be encouraged to play big, live big and dream big."

— **Ivana Han**, Mother of boys, wellness & business mentor

Table of Contents

Introduction 10

Chapter 1 – Veronica's Bookstore 13
Veronica's dreams 14
Matthew's childhood 16
Christmas Eve 18
The mystery unveiled 20
Christmas morning 21
The letter 24

Chapter 2 – A Song about a Boy 29
In the library Archives 30
The Secret Chambers 31
The Big Room 33
Another surprise 33
At the dinner 36
The song about a boy 38

Chapter 3 – The New Day 43
Another dream 46
New chapter in the book 49
Another child in the Archives 52
The joy of reading 55

Matthew's birthday 57

The party 59

Chapter 4 - A Dry Period 63

The fateful day 63

The search for the missing children 65

Not as bad as it seemed 66

What will happen to the library? 67

Renewal of friendship 69

A dry period 71

Chapter 5 - The New Girl 77

At home 79

The next day 82

A surprising turn of events 83

Distressing conversation 85

The principal visits the classroom 87

News about the Secret Chambers 88

Meeting Jasmine again 89

Reunion 90

Chapter 6 - The Old Bookstore 93

The old bookstore 94

The news 97

The dream 98

Decision 100

Reopening 101

About the author 106

Introduction

This book is about a family in an old town that rested on a hill in the north of England. A long time ago it was only a village, but then more houses were built. I first came to visit the town on a cold winter's night. Unfamiliar with the surroundings, I walked slowly, taking it all in. Lanterns on the streets were lit, and I could taste snow in the air, even though there was no snow yet. As I walked, a cold breeze caused a sharp chill to spread all over my body. I followed the Main Street. It curved all the way from the valley below and up towards the hill. The town had a sense of wisdom about it, as if some of its inhabitants carried unique stories with a storyline that one generally finds in books.

Up on the hill only a few houses still had lights on. In the middle of the town was a narrow street with cobbled stones that made it look very old. I turned onto it. Hidden among the houses that lined this street was a bookshop. '*Veronica's Bookstore*' was written in worn letters above the entrance. The window near its door was dark, unwashed, and covered inside with spiderwebs. Peering through the window, I saw that books had been taken off their shelves and left to one side as though no one had been in the shop for months or years.

A little boy carrying a lantern passed me by on that grey hill as if I weren't there. Shivering, he put a hand into his pocket, took out a key, and entered the bookshop. The boy closed the door behind him and left me with a mystery at the time. It seemed that no one else was inside. I wondered how a boy who was not more than eight years old could live in a deserted house like that all on his own. I was about to walk away, when an older gentleman approached and greeted me with a smile. He tilted his hat, showing me respect.

"My grandson walks too fast for me", the gentleman remarked through laughter. I returned the greeting but did not manage to inquire about the bookstore that night.

The boy opened the door for his grandfather so he could join him. As I became acquainted with the boy and spoke with his family over the coming months, the mystery was solved for me. The story that follows is an account of how the first bookstore came to this town.

Chapter 1

Veronica's Bookstore

The town bookstore belonged to Veronica Stone, the boy's grandmother, who from a very early age collected many books, classics and novels alike, all of which she read numerous times. She had developed a love of reading through her parents who spent many winter nights near the fire reading stories to each other. Veronica would snuggle between them and listen as her parents read. Her love for reading made her want to share her books with others and not keep them only for herself. As a child she started coming to the street in front of her parents' house with a box filled with books. She offered them to passersby for free. The pleasure of sharing her love of stories was a suitable payment to this red-head girl. Her long, curly hair, unruly at times, matched her inquisitive personality. Her bright smile made people feel welcome as they passed by. Occasionally older gentlemen and ladies who respected her family would give her a small contribution for the book they took, a few pennies, not much, but the gesture always gladdened Veronica's heart.

Amused at this little girl's passion for reading, Captain Johnston approached her on a dim Saturday afternoon in April of 1925. He was a tall, dark-haired man. He retired from sailing after he injured his leg a number of years ago. Smiling, he gave her two pounds. Twelve-year-old Veronica was shocked when he would not take more than one book — the smallest of them all at that! She looked at Captain Johnston in bewilderment and silently picked up the whole box full of books to give to him. He shook his head. Then he made Veronica an offer that for anyone who was not as humble as that dear girl would be hard to refuse.

Captain Johnston owned an antique shop at the far end of this street. In it were interesting things he collected during his travels throughout the years. He said, "I don't want to buy any books. Instead I want to offer you a table in my shop, so you can start this business of selling books more seriously".

"And the two pounds?", asked Veronica, not understanding why he was paying her.

"That is the payment for renting the table in the shop. Two pounds will cover a full year. After that, your books will probably be in such demand that you may need to look into opening your own shop. There has never been a bookstore in this town, as you know, and most of us love to read." As Captain Johnston said that, he encouraged Veronica with a wink. A long pause filled the air. After a few minutes the Captain said, "So, what do you say? I haven't got all day!"

"Yes, thank you, yes. I would be much obliged to sell books in your store." This was the beginning of Veronica's Bookstore, which became highly acclaimed and much respected among the nobility and the poor alike.

Veronica's dreams

Veronica's family was never rich, though they always had just enough money for food and for new clothes every winter.

This made them luckier than many in their little town. Yet for Veronica, starting a bookstore would normally be out of reach. She never even dreamed of such a thing, though dreaming was not foreign to her young mind. In one of her favourite books, she read about Italy and France. She learned that the small English town on a hill where she lived resembled Italian villages near the Alps. Music in Paris, art in Italy, and homes of English writers fired her lively imagination. She often imagined being an artist who travelled between Paris, Rome, and London. These cities were dream destinations for this little girl.

Even when Veronica was helping her mother cook or doing homework for school, she would suddenly become distant. Her thoughts were taking her to a faraway lands she had never seen. From the books she read, they were as vivid to her as if she did visit them before. "Do the thoughts about foreign countries count as travelling?", she would ask herself. It was not uncommon for her mother, Gillian Stone, to interrupt her in the middle of the most exciting daydreaming: "Veronica, would you stop dreaming and do the cooking? You need to hurry up. Uncle John is coming soon, and you know how restless he can be waiting for his meal".

Gillian was very good at disciplining her daughter, though with balance and charm. She would encourage Veronica in every way. So when Veronica got the offer to sell the books in Captain Johnston's shop, no one was more supportive than her dear mamma. But there was a rule. Veronica's homework needed to be done and all housework for that day completed before she was free to go and sell the books. And Veronica was a good and obedient child. Her life was a little too unadventurous for a child with such vivid imagination.

Veronica was an only child since her younger brother died at birth. The parents had named him Andrew. The family was determined to keep his memory alive. Every November they gathered around the kitchen table, lit a candle to mark Andrew's birth into heaven, and said a prayer for him and other children who died too soon. In this remembering they included all those who died lonely and those whom no one ever prayed for. Afterwards they kept the candle in the living room window, and it burned there, sometimes for weeks. But they never spoke much of that fatal day when death struck their house in this cruel way. Veronica, unaware of the grief that her mother still carried in her chest, would often fall asleep in her parents' arms while they were reading books. She would dream about the stories she heard and make up new ones until the time came to wake up and go to school.

Matthew's childhood

Matthew Alden, Veronica's grandson, grew up in the shadow of her story. He never met her because she died in 1993 when she was eighty, three years before Matthew's birth. But his mother spoke of her mother often. Besides, Veronica was a legend in the town, so Matthew heard many stories about her, most of which were true.

Matthew had short, dark hair, with a few curls resting on his forehead. He had deep blue eyes, and a tender smile. He appeared shy among those he did not know well, but otherwise he had a lively character. Matthew lived with his mother Lucy, father Tom, and grandfather Lewis, Veronica's husband. Like his grandmother, the boy learned to love books, and so he was inspired by the stories that were still being told about her. He always thought she deserved to have a book written about her. It would be a bestseller.

From the day Matthew was born, the first male child in the family after many years, his mother started writing a book about his life, recording stories she did not want to forget. She called it "*A Song about a Boy*". The inspiration came from a song she began singing to him while she carried him for nine months:

> *There is a boy, sweetest of them all.*
> *I carry him beneath my heart.*
> *Soon stars will become shy,*
> *for I hear he has a captivating spark in his eyes.*
> *There is a boy, dearest to my heart.*
> *He keeps growing beneath my heart.*
> *He is my child, and I know a song is growing within his heart.*

Matthew listened to this song throughout the years, so he became very familiar with its tune. Lucy would often hum it as she went about the housework, and on rare nights when she and Matthew were alone, she would sing him the full song and tell a story about her childhood days and about Veronica. Matthew listened to those stories with much interest, trying to imagine what it must have been like to live in the first half of the twentieth century. He wished he had known his grandmother, and he would daydream about conversations the two of them could have had.

One night in 2004 in midwinter, just at the start of the winter holidays, he had the strangest of dreams. *It took place in the winter of 1928, when Veronica was fifteen, seven years older than Matthew's current age. In the dream his grandmother already had her table in the shop for three years and her own shop for just a few months. The original spot that Captain Johnston gave her in his shop had become too small for her growing business. Captain Johnston was getting old, and he decided to leave half of his antique shop to Veronica as her shop. So one summer when she went on a two-week holiday, he hired builders to build a wall in the middle of his shop to divide it in two. He had them build a door that Veronica*

VERONICA'S BOOKSTORE

17

could use to enter her shop. He carved the sign 'Veronica's Bookstore' and put it above her door.

In the dream, Matthew saw Veronica enter the shop, leave her snow-covered coat on the hanger, and start sorting the new books that came in the post. One book seemed to catch her attention. It was "A Christmas Carol" by Charles Dickens. Veronica loved the vivid descriptions in Dickens's writing, though she hadn't yet read this particular book. As Christmas was approaching, she was delighted to be able to read it before she put it for sale. Matthew wanted to talk to her, so in the dream he entered the shop. Soon he realised that Veronica could not see him. He was an onlooker from the future, but she was totally oblivious to it.

Then he heard a voice, yet this was not the voice of a young Veronica but of an old woman. "My dear Matthew, I am your grandmother, Veronica. Every day as you wake up till the time you go to sleep, I am watching over you. I am with you, also imagining conversations that the two of us would have. The good Lord allowed me to tell you this in this dream. You always daydream of knowing me, something you thought impossible since I left this world before you were born. But we do know each other. When the great mystery of time is turned into the eternity, I will embrace you. I offer you an embrace now to carry as a memory within your heart." As Matthew heard these words, he felt a warm embrace around his small shoulders. His grandmother told him one last thing. "Discover the song that is budding within your heart. Listen not only to your mother's song, but listen to your song." At these words he woke up.

Christmas Eve

A few days after Matthew had a dream about his grandmother, it was Christmas Eve. He hadn't told anyone about the dream, which was was more real than an ordinary dream. He didn't want the grown-ups to laugh at him and say it was merely the product of a young child's imagination. Lucy did notice Matthew was more cheerful than usual, but she put it down to Christmastime, which he really loved. Every Christmas Eve the most magic moment for little Matthew was after a light dinner and before Midnight Mass. It was the gift-opening time! He was always first, opening just one gift. Then his mother, father and grandfather would pick a gift to open before it was Matthew's turn again to open another one.

This year, under the Christmas tree he noticed a gift wrapped in an old brown paper and tied with a worn brown ribbon; it had Matthew's name on it. Though this gift wasn't as nicely packaged as the other gifts, something about it attracted him. He felt as if magic were wrapped within this old brown wrapping. He reached his hand towards it and started unpacking. His mother's smile widened as she watched him. When he removed the wrapping, he gasped. It was Charles Dickens's "A Christmas Carol" that belonged to his grandmother, the one he saw in the dream!

"Do you like it?", asked Lucy.

"I . . . I do, very much so. It belonged to Grandmother, didn't it?"

"Yes, it sure did. You guessed it because it looks so old. It was her own personal copy; she never sold it. She said it was too valuable. I wanted you to have it. You are old enough now to read it yourself. I hope you will enjoy it", said his mother.

"Oh, I am sure I will. It was one of her favourite books. This is the book that she got in the post when she was only fifteen, as I saw her in the dream." Matthew gasped when he realised what he said.

VERONICA'S BOOKSTORE

"What dream?", asked Lucy in shock, though she tried to hide it. She had dreams about her mother too, but she thought she was the only one. She wanted to hear all about Matthew's dream.

The mystery unveiled

Matthew was silent for a while, not knowing what to say. He hadn't been prepared to reveal the mystery of that dream, and yet now all of them were looking at him. Tom and Lewis seemed confused as the drama began to be unveiled.

Tom said, "Did you have a dream about your grandmother, Matthew? Come on, explain yourself. Don't be afraid".

"But you will not believe me", he uttered almost through tears. Yet he continued when he saw his mother's encouraging nod to tell her more. "Yes, but it was more than a dream. I think she let me see her world when she was but a young girl, only one scene from one winter afternoon, when she was just starting her own shop. I heard her voice, but I think she was talking from the present, from Heaven. I saw her as a child, as a girl, but she sounded like a grandmother would, old, caring; and she said she is looking after me from above." He said that shyly and then paused to look at Lucy, who had stood up and leaned towards him.

By now she was beaming with a glowing smile, and she gave him a warm kiss on the forehead. "Of course, she is, dear boy. Of course, she is." Matthew felt reassured and no one asked him any more questions that night. They opened more gifts and the cheer of Christmas Eve warmed the room. Yet Matthew could not help but wonder how his mother took his story so well. He expected her to disbelieve him, but she fully affirmed all that he said, even sealing it with the kindness of her motherly kiss.

Later on in the evening, Matthew stayed with Grandfather Lewis, while Matthew's parents went to Midnight Mass. Matthew and Lewis would go to church tomorrow, while Lucy would prepare Christmas dinner and Tom would help her set up the table. They had a very good routine for occasions like Christmas and were a very close family.

As Grandfather was putting Matthew to sleep, the boy asked, "Granddad, did you also have dreams of Grandmother?"

"No, not me. Only your mother and now you. Veronica continues to be as mysterious in death as she was in life, and ever-present too. Your mother has had many dreams where Veronica talked to her, but I will let Lucy tell you about it, in her own time. Now, go and sleep, child. There is a long day ahead of us." He too planted a kiss on Matthew's forehead, and soon after, Matthew sank into a deep restful sleep.

Christmas morning

Matthew woke up to the sound of knocking at the door. It was Rev. Watson, the Anglican minister from the neighbouring parish. Every year before Christmas breakfast he would come bearing gifts. Though the Stones and Aldens were Catholics, they had very good relations with everyone in the area. Every Christmas morning after Morning Prayer, which took place at dawn, Rev. Watson visited some of his parishioners. He would also make a special effort to pay a visit to Matthew's family. They were the only family he visited each year, mostly due to a tradition that his late father started when he was serving in the area.

The strong bond was created through Veronica and her bookstore, because some of her best books were given as gifts

VERONICA'S BOOKSTORE

to the Anglican Public Library in the 1990's. Although Veronica was already old at that time, her passion for spreading a love of reading never ceased. When the library was renovated in 1992, Veronica made a generous offering of a few thousand books from her collection for its reopening. Since then, Rev. Charles Watson and now his son visited Veronica's family every Christmas. Veronica was present only during the first of those visits, as she died a year after, having lived a fulfilled life. The memory of her, however, was as vivid as though she had been present each year.

This year Rev. Watson brought a unique gift with a special request. The gift was an old book from the library, nicely wrapped. Lucy was delighted and intrigued. As she was about to open the gift and satisfy her curiosity, Rev. Watson cautioned her that it was for Matthew. That took her by surprise, not because she was envious, but rather because she did not know what this could mean. Rev. Watson never brought library books for Matthew.

Expectant to see what this Christmas Day would bring, Matthew quickly put his clothes on and rushed downstairs. Not paying too much attention to manners, he completely ignored the fact that a minister was in the living room visiting.

"Hello, little boy", said Rev. Watson as he saw Matthew dashing into the middle of the room. Matthew managed to stop just a second before tumbling into Rev. Watson. He composed himself, smiled as he gave a gentle bow and replied, "Good morning, sir. Very merry Christmas to you!"

The minister laughed heartily and said, "And to you too, dear boy, and to you too!" After a brief pause, he continued, "I have a gift for you with a letter from your grandmother".

Everyone gasped. Lucy tried hard not to faint, and Matthew stood as if someone told him to pretend he was a stone statue and ordered him not to move unless otherwise instructed.

Grandfather Lewis broke the silence with a cheerful comment, "A letter from his grandmother! Well, well, isn't that just what Veronica would do?"

Rev. Watson, seeing slight fear and confusion on Matthew's face, proceeded to explain. "She wrote this letter a few years before her death and asked me to keep it until her grandson or granddaughter, should she have either, would be eight years old. She wanted the letter to be delivered during my Christmas morning visit, together with this book and an invitation to visit the Archives section of the library".

Matthew held the book that Rev. Watson handed to him. It was like waking up from another dream, so it took a few moments before Matthew realised that everyone was waiting for him to open the gift. Even Rev. Watson didn't know which book his grandmother left for him. Matthew carefully removed the packaging and saw a book he heard so much about that he already felt as if he had read it. It was "*The Chronicles of Narnia*" by C. S. Lewis, a beautiful hardbound edition with golden letters embossed on it. "Wow!", gasped Matthew.

Lucy was named after a character from Narnia, and she often told him stories about Aslan and England and adventures that were recorded in that book. He wanted to run to his secret corner in the attic and start reading right this moment, but he knew he couldn't do that. He composed himself, smiled gratefully at the minister, and blushed as his mother looked at him and said, "Your grandmother obviously wanted you to have a very special Christmas this year, my child. Thank Rev.

VERONICA'S BOOKSTORE

Watson for his goodness in keeping this gift for you over the years."

Matthew's eyes rested on the minister's and he simply said, "Thank you for your kindness in making this a very special Christmas for all of us. I am very grateful that Grandmother left this book for me".

"You are very welcome, kind boy", said Watson. "This is the letter that goes with the book. Read it in the evening in peace. Next week we will arrange for you to come with me to the Archives in the library. Another surprise is waiting for you there, but that is all I am allowed to say at this point."

Then looking at Lucy, Tom, and Lewis, he said, "I must hurry. It was lovely to see you as always. Have a very merry Christmas. I shall come by next week to make arrangements for Matthew's visit to the library".

They all said goodbye. Soon the time came for Matthew and Lewis to get ready to go to Christmas Mass, while Lucy and Tom started preparing the dinner.

The letter

The day was spent in a nice warm cheer. As they ate, Grandfather Lewis told the tale of Christmas, about a woman called Mary who was betrothed to Joseph, and how she came to be a God-bearer before their wedding. He spoke of the struggles they faced, of the love they shared, and of the excitement of living out the fulfilment of God's promise. All the while the kettle was boiling on an open fire, so the room was filled with the aroma of burning wood. Lucy would occasionally take the hot water from the kettle and replenish the teapot. After dinner they gathered around the hearth, sang beloved carols, and told stories.

The family was great for telling stories. Though this was usually one of Matthew's favourite moments on Christmas Day, this year he wasn't able to concentrate and listen. His thoughts kept diverting to the letter that was still sitting in the corner of the room, resting on the book. Lucy noticed that Matthew was distracted. She came to sit next to him, cuddled the boy in her arms and whispered, "As soon as Dad and Granddad go for their afternoon rest, you can go and read what Grandmother wrote to you. I will stay to clean here". She pressed a gentle kiss on his forehead and squeezed him closer to herself. She loved this tender little boy with all her heart.

Not long after, Lucy went to the kitchen, and Tom and Lewis went upstairs to rest. Matthew was left alone in the room. His heart started to thump heavily with excitement and yet he didn't move. He looked towards the letter, but he waited. He knew that this was not an ordinary letter. Then he calmly got up and approached the table where the book and letter were. He picked up the envelope, opened it, sat in front of the hearth and started to read.

The letter said:

My dear grandchild,

I wish to tell you that you are very special to me. I prayed for you for many years before your birth. I always had an inkling that I would not meet you on this Earth. I also prayed to the dear Lord to grant my wish to appear in your dream a few days before the Christmas when you would receive this letter. If the Lord has granted me the wish, you will know by now what I am talking about. Heaven and

Earth are knitted together, as you will learn from reading "Narnia". You and I are knitted together, too, not only as a family, but also because God granted me the grace to prepare a way for you by being your grandmother. When I prayed, my dear child, I asked that you would have a song planted in your heart as God breathed His breath of life into you, when you were but a seed of your own being in your mother's womb, growing beneath her heart. Do you know what I am talking about? Can you hear a song within you, even now? Listen, my child, listen. That song is your very life. Listen for now, and later come back and reread what I have written. The words won't leave. Worry not. I ask you to first explore your heart.

And so Matthew put down the letter and listened. There was a song emerging from within him; slowly, silently at first, but sweetly, with tones of delight, joy and harmony with every living being. While he listened, as if birds knew a tale that only creatures of God can tell, they began to sing a song of praise in response.

Chapter 2

The Song about a Boy

Veronica's Bookstore, which was not far from Matthew's home, was no longer open. It had closed in 1990, as Veronica was too unwell to look after it. When Veronica was no longer around to mind the store, the bookstore slowly became like an antique shop that opened on rare dates and special occasions, until it fully closed a few years ago.

As promised, a few days after Christmas, Rev. Watson had arranged for Matthew's visit to the library Archives. The day finally came. Because books were to Matthew what toys were to other boys, he was excited and rather overwhelmed with the happenings of the week.

It was a cold morning, the air was crisp, frost spread on the ground, and the sun shone brightly, turning the frost into glitter. The glow of Christmas lingered on people's lips as they smiled. From the early hours Matthew was so excited that no one could make him eat his breakfast. "I am not hungry, I will eat later", he would repeat eagerly. Eventually Lucy allowed him to skip breakfast.

This morning he had his best clothes on, a suit and a tie. Even though he was only eight he looked like a little gentlemen. He was ready for the mysterious visit to the library. Rev. Watson came very early to pick him up. He guessed Matthew would not be able to sleep much that night.

The library was a short distance away, so they walked. "There is another letter for you that I will give you when we come to the Archives", Rev. Watson explained. He noticed the boy was slightly tense. "There is a part of the library called the Secret Chambers that only your grandmother and myself have known about. Even your parents are not familiar with it. The library staff are aware there is something mysterious about the Archives, but they never knew exactly what that meant. Veronica left special instructions that only her firstborn grandchild is to be escorted into the Secret Chambers. Then it will be up to you to decide if it is to remain a secret, or if we can open it to the public."

"Doesn't Granddad Lewis know of it, either?", asked Matthew in astonishment.

"I think he does know, but your grandmother never admitted telling him", said Rev. Watson, with a wink. "It was our unspoken secret. Veronica shared everything with Lewis, so I am sure he would be familiar with the story about the Secret Chambers. But I doubt he has ever been inside them."

In the library Archives

As they approached the library, Matthew started to breathe deeply. He tried to look calm and respectable, but he was unable to contain all his emotions. Rev. Watson looked at him with a smile, tapped him gently on the shoulder and said, "Don't worry, we are nearly there". In the building, they were escorted by one of the library staff to the far end of the corridor, and then took a lift to the second floor. No one seemed to be around. Perhaps Rev. Watson told people not to disturb them there.

They stepped into a room with a large marble table in the middle of it. On the table was a small envelope, as if forgotten. Matthew raised his eyebrows as if to say, "Should I read it?" Rev. Watson nodded in response to Matthew's inquisitive look. Matthew opened the envelope, his hands shaking a little, and read the letter.

My dear grandchild,

I hope you will like what we are about to show you. I worked on these rooms for more than a decade. We call them Secret Chambers to make them sound more mysterious. Not many people have been past this door that Rev. Watson is about to show you, and you are the first child to go through. After this point my ownership of the Secret Chambers ceases to exist, and it will be solely up to you to decide what to do with it. Take as much time as you need. If your parents ask you what you saw, I suggest you tell them. Not every parent would believe you, but yours will. Good luck. And remember that I am always at your side, watching over you from Heaven.

Matthew took another deep breath, still uncertain as to what to expect. Not wanting to delay, he signalled to Rev. Watson that he was ready and then said, "You can take me to the Secret Chambers".

The Secret Chambers

On the right-hand side of the room were drawers that were filled with details of the books that were kept in the library. Rev. Watson walked to the opposite side that was a bare wall; there was no bookshelf on it or anything else for that matter.

It was as plain as any yellow wall can be. If you looked closer, you would see a lock in the middle of the wall. However, the lock was well hidden, covered with a little piece of yellow metal that blended in with the wall. Rev. Watson inserted the key in the lock and unlocked it. Then he pressed a button that resembled a screw where a picture frame may have been hanging before, and the unusual happened. One small segment of the wall moved away from Rev. Watson, and a few stairs leading downwards appeared. Matthew gaped in astonishment. Rev. Watson started down and called to him, "Follow me".

As they reached the bottom of the stairs, Rev. Watson stepped aside to allow Matthew to go first. Before them lay a corridor, its light already on, giving it a nice warm glow. The corridor was lined on each side with shelves of children's books of all shapes and sizes, colourful books easily reachable for someone who was Matthew's height, or even shorter than that. The corridor circled around, as if resembling railway tracks. Astonishingly, they were rail tracks! A little carrier with a few seats sat in the middle of the track. Matthew entered it, hesitantly at first, but then he relaxed. There was a small handle on the right for navigation. He pushed it and the carrier went forward. Another carrier moved into its place. What a joy! Soon he was driving past thousands of books, in a tunnel, in the heart of the library.

After a short time Matthew reached a big glass door. The carrier slowed down and stopped. "Stand before the door and it will open for you", was written on a golden plaque on the wall. Matthew climbed out of the carrier. He noticed that before the door were the shapes of a small-sized pair of shoes, children's size. He placed his feet onto them and the door opened. He turned around to look for Rev. Watson. The minister was behind him, stepping out of the second carrier and nodding to Matthew to enter. "Go ahead, Matthew, explore."

The Big Room

On a wall at the entrance was written, 'The Big Room'. This wall and the other walls inside were covered in wallpaper that told stories through images that appeared real and in motion. How could this be? Matthew could not tell. The closer Matthew looked, the more he realised that all the images were from only one book, "*The Chronicles of Narnia*".

In the middle of the room a real tree was growing, and around the tree a table was built. A huge fat book lay on top of the table. Matthew removed the clip that kept the book closed and opened the decorated cover. He saw that the book was a very special edition of "*The Chronicles of Narnia*", signed by C. S. Lewis.

"*How did Grandmother manage to get this copy and even have it signed?*", Matthew wondered. Yet soon he forgot the question as he immersed himself in reading. Hours later, or perhaps it was just a few minutes, Rev. Watson entered the Big Room to see how Matthew was doing.

"What do you say? Do you like it?", asked the minister.

"Like it?! It's absolutely incredible! How did you manage to keep this a secret for so long? Were you not tempted to bring your own children here? Did you not want to tell everyone about this amazing place?" But as soon as he said those words, he realised that Rev. Watson's respect for Veronica was such that he would never dare to break his word to her. He had promised to keep the Secret Chambers a secret, and he did. It was as simple as that.

Another surprise

"There is one more thing you haven't yet seen", said Rev. Watson.

Wide-eyed, Matthew stared at him with disbelief. "What more can there be?" he asked, unsure as to what to expect.

Rev. Watson pointed to a door to the right, a door not much taller than Matthew. "The Small Room" was written on the door. The minister said, "The next room is only for children, so you will have to go in on your own and tell me what you find in it. I have never been in that part of the building. It is too small for me".

Matthew opened the door and saw a room dimly lit with the light from the Big Room. It indeed was not very spacious. A child could only take a few steps before reaching the back of the room. There was a chair in the middle, and a little desk was set against the left wall just across from it. A tiny book with a pale brown cover patiently sat on top of the desk. A switch for the light was hanging nearby. Matthew pulled it. When the light came on, his eyes fell on the book. "*Only Children*" was written on the book's cover. Matthew sat down, took the book and started to read.

Rule One

> *Only children and people who are like children can enter into the kingdom of Heaven. Never forget this truth once you grow up. Always remember your childhood wonder, remember the moments you felt love, and treasure also the moments when you learned something new. Remember too the gratitude you felt when you discovered these Secret Chambers and know that this is but an image of what God has prepared for you in this life, and more so in the next. Life is a beautiful adventure if you let it be. Try not to lose your childhood innocence. You can keep it through stories, and this part of the library has many of them. I know you love reading, otherwise you would not be here. Keep reading. Stories will always be your*

*friends and they will help you in your friendships in the
outside world.*

*This is a very short book. In it you will find a few
instructions on how to keep your childlike innocence
alive through the years. I suggest you read only one
chapter each time you come here. Take time to learn
from each instruction and memorise it. Put them into
practice, too. Soon, a few years from now, you will grow
too big to fit in this room and you will tend to forget
what is written inside these pages. But if you decide to
apply these instructions, they will become a part of your
nature and it will be hard to forget them. The first rule
is to keep reading. Reading develops your imagination
and it helps you grow in gratitude about life.*

Matthew read until the end of the page. The voice sounded much
like Grandmother Veronica's. Curious, he turned to the last page,
opened it and found the signature, 'Veronica Stone'. Indeed the
book was written by his grandmother. He wished he had known
her, not only through stories and letters but in reality. If he was
overwhelmed before coming to the library this morning, he was
even more so now that he had discovered the Secret Chambers.
He started to feel hungry. Only now did he realise that he had
not eaten today at all.

He got up from the chair, switched off the light, walked out
of the room and approached Rev. Watson, who was patiently
waiting in the Big Room. The minister wanted to know what
the boy found, but Matthew was unable to speak. It was too
much excitement for his young mind. Rev. Watson had learned
patience throughout the years, so he left the matter until later.
As the two left the Archives, they joined the others who were
now waiting downstairs.

THE SONG ABOUT A BOY

At the dinner

A special dinner was organised in the library. One of the conference rooms on the ground floor had been transformed into a proper dining room. This was not part of Veronica's instructions, but Rev. Watson thought a dinner would be a good way to end Matthew's special visit to the library Archives. On a large table in the middle of the room was a festive tablecloth and plates of various sizes and stylish cutlery. Wine glasses were spread around the table. Decorating the room were candles burning in candlesticks and flower arrangements. As soon as people entered, they could feel warmth and a spirit of friendship enfolding them. The whole atmosphere was cheerful and welcoming.

Lucy, Tom, and Grandfather Lewis were already seated at the table, together with some of the library staff and a few distinguished guests. They were engrossed in a conversation about some recent happenings from their town, so they didn't immediately notice when Matthew arrived with Rev. Watson. Lucy spotted them first. As her little boy ran into her arms, her face turned radiant. Before she managed to ask him how the day went and what the secret actually was, Matthew buried his face into his mother's chest and started to cry. She held him tighter, lifted him up and took to the side of the room where they could have some privacy. She was slightly afraid something bad had happened, but her intuition told her Matthew was merely overwhelmed. For no matter how wonderful the news and all the gifts were, it was all quite too much for his little heart.

After a good cry, Matthew relaxed and smiled. "Grandmother left me the children's part of the library. In it rail tracks lead to a Big Room and a Small Room that have surprises in them. Going there was so much fun!" His eyes glowed as he spoke, then his expression changed again, looking rather sad. "I just wish I knew her, really knew her, not only through letters and stories. Why did she have to die before I was born?"

Lucy gently kissed her boy on the forehead and wiped the remaining few tears from his face. There was nothing she could say to soothe his longing for his grandmother or really answer his question. She held him close. Then she whispered, "Even though I knew her, I miss her too. Let's focus on all the good you experienced today. Come, it's time for dinner. Everyone is waiting to hear what you saw, and I want to know what you mean by the Big Room and the Small Room, and the library with rail tracks". They smiled and went back to the table.

"So tell us, what did that mysterious woman leave for you to see? We have been here for hours waiting to hear what she put in those Archives", said Lewis with excitement in his voice. Matthew sat between his mother and Grandfather Lewis and started telling what happened during the day. Everyone listened in bewilderment, especially the library staff who were coming here for years totally unaware of the treasures that the Archives held.

For as long as the boy was speaking, silence was palpable in the dinning room. "What books were in those Archives that the library does not yet have? How did the railway tracks work? What did it all look like?" These and other questions were popping into people's minds, but no one dared to interrupt the boy lest he forget to say some important detail. When Matthew finished the story about his explorations, a chatter broke the silence. Most of the guests wanted to leave the dinner table in order to go and see the children's library for themselves.

Rev. Watson cleared his throat and spoke, "No one is going to the Archives today, apart from those of us who have already been.

Veronica left a clear instruction that Matthew should decide what is to happen to the children's library. Should he still decide to keep it hidden from the public and explore it on his own, he can. Whatever he will decide he needs to do freely. Today is not a time for that decision. He has had enough to deal with for one day."

That settled the matter. The food was soon brought to the table and the conversation returned to the everyday matters.

Lucy leaned towards Matthew, squeezing his hand, and said in a low voice, "We'll talk more later. I would like to hear more".

"Of course, I will tell you all about it", said Matthew. "I am hungry now. I have not eaten anything the whole day. I must tell you about the railway tracks! I would like to show you everything too. But don't tell anyone that yet."

When they got home that evening, Matthew was already falling asleep. Tom carried him into the house and placed him in the bed. "He has had a lot of excitement today", said Tom to Lucy. The two of them stayed up late that night, talking about what had happened. Lucy also spoke about the song she used to sing, the one she called 'The Song about a Boy".

The song about a boy

"Are you still writing the book about him?", asked Tom.

"Yes, though not as often as before. I also call it *"The Song about a Boy"*. I did write about this Christmas, and in the next few days I want to write about today."

"I still hear you humming that song", affirmed Tom with a lot of love in his voice. "Sing it to me now. I love hearing your voice, and that song is like a prayer for our little boy. Will you sing it to me now?"

Of course, she would. Even had he asked something harder she would obey. Not as a task, but out of her love for this wonderful man who made her his wife.

There is a boy, sweetest of them all.
I carry him beneath my heart.
Soon stars will become shy,
for I hear he has a captivating spark in his eyes.
There is a boy, dearest to my heart.
He keeps growing beneath my heart.
He is my child, and I know a song is growing within his heart.

Her voice filled the room, and memories of her pregnancy flooded her mind. She sang the song a few times and then stopped. Tears started rolling slowly down her face. Tom kissed her cheeks unaware of what stirred Lucy's heart. She told him, "Remember how I could not conceive for a while and then when I was in the fourth month there was a scare that the baby would not survive? I think it was around that time that I started singing this song, and Matthew was fine".

"I will never forget those days. I remember it every time I put Matthew to sleep, looking at his calm face dreaming the unknown dreams", said Tom. "When you gave birth, I was the happiest man on earth. That's why days like today are even more meaningful and more precious than what they appear to be on the surface. Our little boy is a gift, and I love that we can show him how grateful we are that he is with us."

"Do you think he has a song rising within his heart?", asked Lucy.

"You will have to ask him that. His life is a song whether he knows it yet or not."

That is not quite what she meant, but they understood each other even when words failed to express their thoughts. Even if things were left unsaid, they somehow communicated them beyond words, as if speaking heart to heart.

Tom said, "Your mother Veronica, I never understood her, but she was some woman. How did she manage to prepare all these gifts and secrets for him when she is not even among us any longer?" He pondered out loud.

Tom and Lucy leaned against each other in silence, grateful for each other, for life, for the boy that grew within each of their hearts. Then they fell asleep, night covering them gently until the morning woke them up again with fresh stories for a new day.

Chapter 3

The New Day

A few weeks after the visit to the library Archives, Matthew was back at school. He decided he would not speak about what happened over Christmas in any great detail. His main reason was that some children in his class were poor. He did not want them to feel bad that he had a wonderful adventure when they might not have had gifts or enough food at Christmas. He would like to invite those children to be the first to come and see the Secret Chambers, but he did not know how to do it without offending others, so he chose to wait. His mother always told him not to rush with decisions. Things become clearer when you give them time. So that's what he did.

Matthew went to the Archives weekly, partly out of curiosity, partly because he wanted to read Grandmother's book in the Small Room. Sometimes Lucy came with him, sometimes Tom, but he enjoyed it the most when Granddad joined him because Lewis would tell him stories about Grandmother that were not so well-known.

One day Lewis was sitting with Matthew in the Big Room after they had explored some of the books along the railway track. Granddad said, "One time I wouldn't read the book that Veronica wanted me

VERONICA'S BOOKSTORE
43

to read, and she became annoyed at me. I hadn't really realised how important it was to her that I read it until I learned what that book was. She normally let me pick my own books to read. Heh, that time was different. You know what the book was? It was the one you came to read today. The one she wrote. She only wrote three books in her lifetime. Ha, three that I know of", he said with a laugh. "I would not be surprised if next Christmas she sends us some unknown unpublished work that none of us knew existed."

The boy looked astonished and almost afraid at the mention of another Christmas surprise. "I am just joking child", Lewis said. He gently embraced Matthew and ruffled his hair before he continued. "Anyway, where was I? Ah yes. Of the three books she wrote, "*Only Children*" was her favourite one."

"You read it Granddad?"

"Yes, I did, child. When I realised she wanted me to read one of her books, I obeyed without delay. She had a way with words, not only the written word. I loved listening to her. And she wanted me to tell her my honest opinion about the book. But my honest opinion was that her work was always excellent — because it was. She thought I was teasing her, when in fact I only told the truth." You could hear nostalgia in his voice. He missed her, though he did not like to admit it.

"She knows now, Granddad. She can see you from Heaven and hear what you are saying. She knows now."

Lewis smiled at Matthew, "Indeed she does, my dear boy. Thank you. You know, you remind me of her; she never lost her innocence. The lessons she wrote in that book, she practiced regularly and never tired of being goodhearted, like you. Go now and read more in the book, and then we will go home. It's almost dinner time".

Matthew got up, went into the Small Room and put on the light. He picked up Veronica's book, sat in the chair, and started to read. Sometimes he would reread the rule he already read, in order to savour the book longer, but also to remember the words better. Today he read another chapter.

Rule Two

The second rule to keep your childhood innocence, my dear child, is to laugh a lot. There is always something funny in life, but you have to learn to look at life that way. It is about the attitude you have and how you see things. You cannot always be positive, of course. Life is hard as well, as you will learn soon. We all do. Life spares no one. But you can always try to have a little bit of humour in your heart; it will lighten up some of the difficult days and give you joy and enthusiasm during the good ones. This will also bring joy to others. And how do you learn a joyful attitude? By practicing it. It's not only in laughter that joy is expressed, it also comes out through thoughts and actions. Sometimes even a person's presence can bring joy, as I am sure you would have learned from your mother.

Here Matthew stopped reading. How does she know that mother brings me joy? He had come to know Grandmother through the stories about her and above all through her own voice, so he concluded that she would most likely answer that question. He kept reading and found that he was right.

You may wonder why I mention your mother. It is simply because she brought me joy, even when she was a child. She would enter a room, bringing a flower she had picked outside, and her whole face became a radiant smile.

Yes, he recognised that. His mother often shone with joy when she was talking to him, or when he did something that delighted her heart. He understood without a doubt what Grandmother meant by saying that someone's presence can bring joy. He wondered if his presence did that too. He got carried away in his thoughts forgetting to read until Granddad called him, "Are you there?"

"Yes", Matthew replied. "I will be out soon. I am not finished yet." He read the rest of the page.

She did not do that deliberately, knowing she was going to bring me joy. She was just being herself. Your mother had a natural inclination to find joy in everyday moments, in details of life, and she did so with great love. Another good thing was that she wanted to share that joy. I must say she delighted my heart every single day. You too can find what brings you joy, practice it daily, and share it with people. Then, your presence will also become one that captivates others with joy and appreciation of life.

Matthew closed the book, gave a deep sigh, and went out of the room. It was dinner time.

Another dream

When Matthew and Granddad got home, dinner was already on the table. The chatter at the table was very joyful as each member of the family spoke about how their day went. Lucy asked Matthew about his visit to the library, and this time he

told her about the book [...]
excitement; but she also looked [...]
of this book or that she is mention [...]
hid it well. Later that evening, when M[...]
sleeping, Lucy spent some time in the liv[...]
fire, thinking of her little boy. That night Luc[...]

She saw herself as a very small child in the old comp[...]
the family house where she grew up. Her mother was re[...]
a bedtime story. In the dream, even when Lucy was already [...]
her mother kept reading from a set of worn out papers that r[...]
something profound scribbled on them. 'Scribbled' because a lot of
the writing was crossed over with different coloured pens and notes
were made on a side. The pages were a bit of a mess. Yet her mother
read without interruption because she knew the text quite well. The
book was called "Only Children" ...

In the dream when Lucy woke up and her mother was still reading,
she asked, in her long-forgotten childhood voice, "Have you been here
all the time, all through the night, without sleeping yourself?"

"No, child. I woke up before you and continued reading where I
stopped last night. You will remember the lessons even if you don't
recollect listening. I have been reading this book to you for such a
long time that I believe it will become your second nature. As I make
changes in the book, I read you the new version."

Then, all of a sudden, the voice of her mother changed, becoming older,
much older, as if from a time right before she died. Now she addressed
the grown-up Lucy. She said, "My dear Lucy, I wanted to prepare the
Archives for you when you were still a child. I had longed to show
you something as magnificent then, but until I was old enough to
know how to do what I wanted to do, you grew up. I delighted in you
more than I ever was able to show you, like you delight in your child as

THE NEW DAY

*ns where I can visit
vhile.*

*to know so that you
in his dreams. I will
ide to tell me not to
ig favour. I can keep
ısk for it to stop, then
en. I have only three
ɔre I will have to say
ır, until Christmas. I
. You are a wonderful
n above. I know you
am always with you,
my child.*

Veronica paused for a moment, and then continued. "One last thing. Don't be afraid to ask Matthew about his song. He may need an encouragement to explore it, to let it emerge from within him. Perhaps the song has already started coming out of his heart. If so, it will help him understand it if you talk to him. There is no one better to help him with that than you."

At that, Lucy woke up. As soon as she opened her eyes, the sunshine beaming through the window made her close them again for a short while. She relaxed, letting the sunshine wash over her face. She took a deep breath and then gave a little sigh. She waited a few moments to absorb her dream before getting up. As she rose from bed, she noticed that the curtains blocked off some sunshine and created a beautifully shaped shadow on the wall, a pattern of light and darkness. It made her think how life will always have both, and that maybe this realisation is what makes us appreciate the connection with those we love even more.

She missed talking to her mother when she was alive. While those dreams brought comfort, she also felt alone in having them. Tom and Lewis tried to understand; however, the experience was foreign to them. Matthew was the only one who would understand, but she could not burden him with this particular dream. Not yet.

New chapter in the book

After the dream Lucy realised why the book Matthew mentioned was so familiar to her. "*Only Children*" was in the making when she was small, and Veronica read a number of versions of each chapter to her as she was writing them. Lucy had totally forgotten this! Even now she was not sure if she remembered it, or she simply learned it from the dream.

That morning Matthew got ready for school, and Lucy arranged to pick him up later. Once a month she volunteered at the library, helping children from impoverished areas to learn to read. They played games as they learned, and the children loved it. Matthew often came with her after school and played with them. Today Lucy gave him permission to visit the Archives instead, because Matthew would not have time to come to the library for the next ten days. He would have to spend time preparing for exams.

After school Lucy collected Matthew. They walked to the library, which was not far from the school. Because they arrived a little early, Lucy had time to go with Matthew to the Big Room. Upon entering the Secret Chambers, they went into the carrier on the rail tracks and drove there. Lewis was already in the Big Room, reading the newspaper, ready to spend the time with Matthew while Lucy conducted the reading class. Lucy joined her father for a short while. Matthew went exploring neighbouring shelves before entering the Small Room in order to lose himself in reading Veronica's book.

When Matthew turned to the next chapter in *"Only Children"*, he saw a small golden key on the left-hand side; text began on the right. The key seemed to be carved into the page, so it was not noticeable until this chapter was opened. The dainty key looked as if it could unlock secrets long forgotten, perhaps even centuries old. Matthew began to read the chapter,

Rule Three

This key is a key of forgotten dreams. Many people forget their dreams when they grow up. They forget what was stored in their hearts when innocence was still speaking to them of the possibilities that are ahead. Children have imagination. If this imagination is nurtured into adulthood, it will help them deal with difficult situations. Creativity is a great skill to have in life, in relationships, in life's ups and downs. Creativity that comes from deep within your heart is what I encourage you to nurture every day of your life.

Remember this key, take it in your hands, and feel its touch on your skin. It may feel cold at first, but as you hold it a little while longer, it becomes warm, as if it speaks that it can unlock any door. This key gives you hope. Hope, my dear child, is a treasure in this world. Some people, as they grow old, lose hope. It's as though they forget to live, and years go past. But this key leads them directly into their hearts, into their most sacred dreams. The key awakes hope, and after a long time the once hopeless people feel alive again. You, however, can be careful never to forget what your heart holds inside. Some things will become revealed only later, when you will be able to understand them. But it is crucial that you keep this key — the memory of it — as it will remind you of the dreams you have that are your birthright. This key and the hope it holds will help you choose the right path.

You will encounter cynicism in the world around you. People will tell you to forget your dreams. Don't let them fool you. No matter what you hear from the outside, know that your heart stores treasures and dreams; some of them are not only good for you, but for others too. This third rule to keep your innocence may be one of the harder lessons in this book: Hold onto the dreams of your heart and the hope you embraced as a child. When you do this, you fan hope in other peoples' hearts and help them to treasure the dreams they had as a child.

This was a complicated rule, Matthew thought. He did not even know what his dreams were. How can he lose something he does not yet know? As he was thinking about his dreams, he accidentally turned the next page, even though the book instructed him to read chapter by chapter, not rushing ahead. That page was empty. This made him curious, so he opened the other page after that one, and another one, and another. All the other pages seemed empty. Empty! How could they be empty? He did not understand.

Instead of getting upset, he decided to read the third rule again. He turned the pages back to that rule and read *"This key, and the hope it holds will help you choose the right path"*. He removed the key from the page, held it in his hand, and wondered how

THE NEW DAY

it could tell him the right path. Perhaps the key would remind him to take the road that was really his to take. Something about the sentence he reread resonated with him. He kept repeating it. There was something he wanted to do. Maybe this would help him to make a decision about it.

Matthew closed the book, switched off the light above the desk, and went out to see his granddad. Lewis and Lucy were already waiting for him. He wanted to tell them what he had read, but as they seemed preoccupied, he decided to leave it till another time.

Another child in the Archives

At home during dinner, Lucy noticed Matthew was unusually silent. "What is the matter, my dear child?," she asked with tenderness in her voice.

"Mum, I'm bothered about something."

She smiled warmly, encouraging him to go on. "About what, my dear?", said Lucy.

Matthew continued, "The book I told you about, the one Grandmother wrote. The chapter I read today was about not forgetting our dreams, and there was a small key in the page before I started to read. Grandmother said that this key would help me choose the right path. The key is important. It made me think of something. So far I am the only child who has ever been in the Archives, I mean in the Big Room and in the Small Room. But there are so many books there. It is not right that I keep them to myself. I don't feel good about it. But I don't want to make them public either". He sighed. "I fear people would ruin them, not take care of them the way they deserve."

Suddenly he had an illumination and his eyes glistened. "Maybe I could bring one other child to see the Secret Chambers though. Only one. What do you think?" He waited in expectation for Lucy's answer.

Her smiled reassured him that his idea was not strange or unwelcome. "Is there someone you had in mind?", asked Lucy.

Matthew wrinkled his forehead and thought for a moment. His face became serious briefly, before it lightened up again. "Yes", he said, "Tommy McGuinness, the boy who comes to your class to learn to read. He seems to really like books. His mother and two sisters are always joyful, and they are grateful that Tommy enjoys his reading class. The family is poor but so selfless. I . . . I . . . really like that. I don't know them well, but I like them. I wouldn't want Tommy to have an experience that separates him from his sisters, so maybe one time they can all come. But for the first time I would like to invite him alone. I think he would really enjoy it. Would his mother and the rest of his family allow him to have an adventure that he could not fully tell them about immediately?"

"Well, I do not know. We will have to ask them", answered Lucy. "They will need to know something, his mother at least, so that she can feel safe letting him go for an hour on his own with you. I think we can try to organise it one evening after the reading class. I will ask Rev. Watson to have a little bit of food prepared for the rest of the family while Tommy goes up to the Secret Chambers with you. Dad and I can entertain the family, and Granddad can look after you and Tommy as you explore the Secret Chambers."

"That would be wonderful!", said Matthew, excited. "When can we do it?"

THE NEW DAY

"Perhaps next month", said Lucy. "Tommy's mother comes to the library weekly herself. She takes a class in English classics there. I saw her a few times. I know the days when that class is held. I will go to the library later this week and try to talk to her. I will explain that your grandmother left you a gift that you want to keep private from the public, but that you would like to show to some children. I will tell her that we were wondering if Tommy may be the first to come and see it. His mother is a kind, noble woman; I am sure she will not gossip about it. If she agrees, we'll arrange for Tommy to join you next month after reading class."

And that is how it happened. It was February 2005. Tommy had learned to read quite well over the last year. When he started the class, he was already proficient enough, but some of the more difficult words caused him problems. He had mastered them by now, and both Lucy and Tommy's mother were proud of his progress. Lucy was also proud of Matthew's tender heart, because he had chosen a fine boy who would really appreciate the Secret Chambers to be the first little visitor from outside the family. Tommy was very excited, especially because he did not know what to expect. Matthew knew how that felt; at Christmas he did not know what to expect either. Lucy noticed that Tommy found it hard to concentrate during the class, but that was only natural.

After the class, Tommy and Matthew had tea and biscuits before Lewis took them upstairs. They were talking about the books they each read. The conversation helped Tommy to relax. As the boys were on their way to the library Archives, they both felt a new friendship had started to form. Some friendships begin in youth, before the maturing of age, and they never end. Even when hair turns grey and tales are retold many times as if viewed on old photographs, these friendships remains. This was to be one of them.

The joy of reading

When they reached the Secret Chambers, Tommy started to breathe with difficulty. Matthew got scared. He thought Tommy may have asthma and might need medication to help him breathe. "Do you have asthma?", Matthew asked.

Tommy took a few deep breaths and said, "No, I don't have asthma. Not that I know of anyway. I just never had something this exciting happen in my life. I don't think I know how to handle it".

Lewis reached into the cupboard at the entrance, found a glass, filled it with water from a drinking fountain nearby and offered it to the boy. "There, my dear fella, drink this", said Lewis. "Soon you will be distracted with books and imagination and there will be no thinking about how to react. I understand this is overwhelming. It has been for all of us. Take it easy. We won't go in until you are ready. There is no rush."

Tommy drank water as if his life depended on it and said, "It's ok now. Thank you. I think I am ready".

And so they entered the Secret Chambers. What excitement! The rail tracks and carriers looked more fascinating to Tommy than if they stepped into a scene from a film. Tommy and Matthew went into one carrier, and Lewis took the one after them. The carriers stopped at the entrance into the Big Room and the boys got out. Matthew had Tommy step onto the small shoe prints in front of the glass door and it swung open. As Tommy looked in, he exclaimed, "Wow! Your granny left you all this?!"

Matthew looked a little embarrassed. He did not like to think he had more than others, even though in this case it was true. "Yes", he said shyly.

"Thank you for sharing it with me!", said Tommy as he ran inside and feasted his eyes on all the books. He stopped in front of *"The Chronicles of Narnia"* on the table and looked at it with reverence. As he opened the book, he started sobbing. He sat at the chair that was nearby and started to read. Matthew and Lewis did not know why he was crying, but they understood. *"When you are overwhelmed, sometimes tears can say it better than words, until you are able to speak"*, thought Matthew, remembering his tears when he was in the Secret Chambers for the first time.

After ten minutes, Tommy calmed down. He stopped reading and looked up with a soft smile on his face. He said, "My father used to read me this book when I was younger. I did not know how to read at the time. He read all the seven books, twice. It took more than a year. I remember I had a very vivid imagination, and so I could see the whole story as if it happened in front of me while he read. This was my favourite time every day; coming home from school to a warm house, my family sitting around the hearth and my father reading this book to us. My mother would make tea and prepare dinner. We would stop reading in order to eat, and then come back around the fire afterwards, and Father read again".

Tommy paused for a moment, and then continued. "My father died two years ago. I miss him every day. When he realised he was ill, he made an effort to spend even more time with me and my sisters. He instructed us about life, about kindness, friendship, love for Mother and one another, and gratitude for simple things. He made sure to create memories with him. We spent so much time together that we remember him well to this day. I am very grateful to him for making sure that we enjoyed his presence for as long as we could."

"After he died, my mother continued reading Narnia to us. She wanted us to remember Father. Today reading the book he read to us reminds me of that time we spent together. That is why I cried. I am sorry if I made you uncomfortable or scared you. I am grateful to you, too, for giving me this experience."

Matthew and Lewis reassured him that it was okay to cry.

The three of them ended up talking for hours around the book, reading, laughing, reminiscing about people they love from their past, and being grateful for people in their life now. Lucy came to say that Mrs. McGuinness was still downstairs and would wait as long as needed. They did not need to rush. That was good to know. The boys have forgotten anyone was waiting for them outside of the world of the Secret Chambers. Time had stopped, and for a few moments they were in a reality of their own. They did not visit the Small Room. That would wait for some other time.

Matthew's birthday

A few weeks passed. Tommy went with Matthew to the Secret Chambers almost on a weekly basis. His sisters, however, managed to visit only once. Not that they were unwelcome. They were invited every time, but they had other activities they wanted to go to. Matthew made sure that they did not feel left out and they did not. He enjoyed deepening his friendship with Tommy. Lucy and Mrs. McGuinness, whose first name was Clara, became quite fond of each other as well.

It was the end of March. Spring slowly started to come to England with buds bursting on bushes, trees turning green and flowers opening up. Lucy was singing her *song about a boy* as Matthew's birthday was approaching in April. Matthew asked not to be given anything new. He felt he received his birthday gift at Christmas and did not want his family to spend money on him. Besides, the happenings around Christmas were quite overwhelming. He wanted something much less exciting. He was grateful for every gift he was ever given, but he could not bear more strong emotions. The excitement when the Secret Chambers were revealed a few months back was enough. His birthday wish was to gather with his favourite people, old and new, in the Big Room in the Secret Chambers that Grandmother created for him before he was even born.

The big day came, 9th April 2005. Matthew was going to be nine. In the morning Lucy prepared his favourite breakfast, eggs with brown toast and a warm glass of milk. It was Saturday, so the get-together could be scheduled early, at two o'clock in the afternoon. Lucy planned to let Matthew sleep a little longer, but he was awake unusually early and very cheerful.

"I dreamt about Grandmother!", Matthew said to Lucy, beaming with happiness. "She wished me a happy birthday and read from a book in my dream. This was a different book from the one I have been reading in the Small Room. I don't remember much of the book, only that it was interesting. Something about the dream seemed different. I don't know if I dreamt about her as you usually dream — about things that happen in your day or things you think about a lot or if she spoke to me directly, as she did a few times before. What do you think, Mum?"

"I could not tell for sure, darling", said Lucy. "But I am certain she would want to wish you a happy birthday. Did she sound the same as in previous dreams?" Lucy tried not to let her own recent dream influence this conversation. She was happy Matthew was happy. But she was also a little sad that her mother would not be able to make her son beam with such happiness for much longer. However, she did her best to hide the sadness and not think of it too much herself. The important thing was that today on his birthday he was happy.

Matthew tried to recall if Grandmother sounded the same or different this time. He could not tell. He and Lucy agreed that Veronica would want to wish him a wonderful day, regardless if she really said it or if he imagined it. They decided to leave the topic of the dream for now. Matthew enjoyed his breakfast, and then started to get ready for the party.

The party

All the guests started to gather in the Secret Chambers from the early afternoon. Matthew's family was there first, soon joined by Rev. Watson, his wife Sarah, and daughter, Elizabeth. The Reverend also had a son, but he was out of town at this time. Then Tommy arrived with his two sisters and his mother, Clara. Matthew was told that there was still one more guest to arrive. Not knowing anything about this guest, he tried not to appear too anxious. Lucy, however, noticed it and reassured him, "Don't worry. I think you will be pleased when this mystery guest comes".

A few minutes later, at the door of the Secret Chambers a little girl appeared. She walked in accompanied by Rev. Watson's wife Sarah, who met her at the entrance to the library. The girl, whose name was Nika, looked a little timid, which was understandable. The only information she had received was that she was invited to a party for a boy named Matthew in a place that not many knew existed. Her parents had been notified about all the details, and because they knew Matthew's family, they were confident it was safe to let her attend the party.

Tommy had suggested that Lucy invite Nika. The sweet girl was from Matthew's class. Tommy knew Matthew liked her and would want to show her the Secret Chambers. Matthew did not *like her* the way boys like girls, because that would be new to him. He was not used to that yet. He did like something about her, though. Knowing Nika was often on her own, he told Tommy how he wanted her to see the Secret Chambers. Matthew always wanted to make people happy, especially if it seemed like they might not know much happiness.

Matthew's face broke into a smile when he saw Nika, and he run towards her to welcome her and introduce her to others. Recognising him, she responded with a smile.

Matthew was always kind to her, even though up to now they have not actually been friends. Now she felt less apprehensive about being among strangers and visibly relaxed.

The party was warm and cheerful. The guests told anecdotes from Matthew's childhood, shared various funny and wise stories with each other, enjoyed the finger food Rev. Watson organised, and naturally they remembered Veronica, Matthew's grandmother. Everyone marvelled at the Secret Chambers, grateful they could be together there, celebrating the good things in life. Matthew, Tommy and Nika spent some of the time in the Small Room. It was little tight there for all three of them, but they had a good laugh over it. Matthew read one of the chapters of "*Only Children*" out loud. This was the day when all of them were happy, a day Matthew would remember for a long time.

Chapter 4

A Dry Period

After Matthew's birthday, things went back to normal. Everyone had enjoyed the party, and Matthew had gained a new friend, Nika. Tommy continued with the class that Lucy was teaching in the library, and Mrs. McGuinness became her close friend. Lucy preferred to call Tommy's mother Mrs. McGuinness. This was not because of age, as Clara was only a few years older than Lucy, but because there was something noble about this woman, and Lucy wanted to acknowledge that. Clara found this most embarrassing, so Lucy made an effort to address her by her first name instead.

Since the party, the children enjoyed spending time with one another. Nika became a regular visitor to the Secret Chambers. Hardly a day would pass that she would not join Tommy and Matthew in their adventures. Rev. Watson was delighted that the Secret Chambers were in constant use at last. The children all got along very well . . . until one fateful day when something unexpected happened.

The fateful day

It was a late April morning. Lewis was sitting in the kitchen after breakfast about to read the newspaper. As soon as he set eyes on the headline, he turned pale. It was good that no one else was around, as they would get a fright thinking he had suddenly become unwell. He drank water to cool himself and continued reading. When he finished, he made sure to fold the newspaper and put it away so that Matthew did not see it. He decided to go out for a walk and to look for Rev. Watson on the way. Even after a good hour passed walking in fresh air, Lewis was still upset. It was not like him to be that way.

Matthew was in school at the time, and he had arranged to go to the Secret Chambers with Nika afterwards. Tommy was to join them an hour later, because he first had to help one of his sisters with housework after school.

Later on, in the Big Room, Matthew and Nika were reading "*The Chronicles of Narnia*" when they heard a strange noise. It resembled the sound of a key locking the door and a few voices echoing in the distance. It soon became quiet again, so they paid no attention to the noise. As often happened in the land of Narnia or when children were playing together, they forgot about time. So an hour after Tommy was supposed to arrive, they still hadn't noticed that he wasn't there.

Tommy had arrived, shortly after the other two heard that noise, but he could not get in. The door into the Secret Chambers was locked. He heard Matthew and Nika talk and laugh from a distance and concluded they decided not to let him join this time. He called Matthew's name, but the corridor with the rail tracks was too long for his voice to carry over and to the other side of the glass door.

Tommy did not realise, and neither did Matthew and Nika, that one of the library staff locked the Secret Chambers, unaware that anyone was inside. Everyone who loved the library was quite concerned about the morning news. Most of them acted with only half of their usual attention, as the other half was filled with worry.

The search for the missing children

Lucy presumed that Matthew went home after school. On arriving home, she was quite surprised and worried when she found that the house was empty. Lewis was still out. She did not think Matthew would have gone to the library, for she assumed he would have heard the terrible news at school. Everyone was talking about it. Tom soon joined her at home, and now both were concerned. They asked a few of their neighbours if anyone had seen Matthew, but no one had.

Before deciding to call the police, Lucy phoned Clara to check if maybe Matthew was there. It was not like him to go somewhere without notice. But it was a kind of a day when hardly any of them behaved as usual. The news had unsettled everything.

Clara answered the phone and as soon as she heard Lucy say, "We can't find Matthew", she exclaimed, "But he is in the Secret Chambers! Tommy went there. The entrance door was locked, and Tommy presumed he was not welcome today. He is in quite a state, and nothing I say will reassure him that he must have been mistaken thinking that. His friends would never have shut him out".

Lucy gasped, "In the Secret Chambers? Oh, Matthew has not heard the news. The whole library must be closed by now. If he is there with Nika, they must both be terrified. I am sure they tried to leave by now. If he is on his own, even worse. Thank you, Clara. I will contact Rev. Watson immediately and go to rescue Matthew". After Clara hung up the phone, she could not get the words "to *rescue* Matthew" out of her head. Rescue from what?

A DRY PERIOD

Rev. Watson was already on his way to the library because someone had notified him that Matthew was missing. He knew that there was only one place where the boy could be. Meanwhile, Nika and Matthew started to worry when Tommy never came. They became even more concerned when Lewis did not arrive to pick them up. Matthew often went to the Secret Chambers on his own, but he would always be accompanied home. Because the children had no reason to think that something was amiss, they continued playing, telling themselves that someone must be already on their way to take them home. Matthew and Nika heard the same kind of noise again; it was a key in the door. It was similar to the sound they heard hours before. They were both slightly afraid, but neither wanted to admit it. They stood there, waiting.

Not as bad as it seemed

Rev. Watson unlocked and opened the door to the Secret Chambers and saw the light coming from the Big Room. This put him at ease, almost completely. He rode a carrier to the glass door and called for Matthew. The boy joyfully responded and burst through the door with Nika close behind. He rushed towards Rev. Watson and embraced him forcefully. Matthew had not realised how scared he had been until he saw a friendly face. He had tried to be strong both for himself and for Nika, but he was still a boy and was glad to see Rev. Watson coming to take them home. When the fear dissipated even more, Matthew wondered why Tommy and Lewis hadn't appeared but Rev. Watson did.

"What happened today?", asked Matthew. Rev. Watson replied, "I will tell you in a minute, child. Just let me call your mother to tell her you and Nika are safe and that I will bring you both home straight away".

After he had phoned both Matthew's and Nika's parents, he told the children, "A fire started in one part of the library late at night. Thankfully, it was stopped soon after it was noticed, but the public did not know that. We did not notify the papers about the fire since we did not wish to cause panic by mentioning anything until we examined the damage today. But the news already went out, as the news does, and the whole town was in panic. People thought the library was going to burn down".

"We closed early today", Rev. Watson continued, "so one of the library staff must have locked you in when you were here playing. I am not sure how no one saw you coming in, as they would have told you not to stay long. I am upset that they did not check if anyone was left behind, but I think everyone was in the state of a shock. This only means we need to review our closing up and fire drill policies. We have had some financial difficulties too, and we may need to close one part of the building until who knows when."

Rev. Watson was deeply concerned that the children were left behind, but relieved to know they were both safe and he could bring them home unharmed.

Matthew was most concerned with one thing he heard: "We may need to close one part of the building until who knows when". What did that mean? And what did that mean for the Secret Chambers?

What will happen to the library?

Lucy was relieved Matthew was safe. She prepared warm milk for him and made sure to talk to him in case he was upset. Lewis was also home and looked a little better now that he knew that the library had not burned down. But he was still concerned, though not as much as in the morning. He apologised to Matthew for being so distressed that he forgot to let him know not to go to the library that day.

No one really knew what it meant that part of the library may have to close. The family sat around the kitchen table and discussed this day and how they each were affected by it. This was one of their strengths; they spoke about everything.

Matthew looked sad. Not only was he worried about the Secret Chambers but he felt bad that Tommy thought that he did not wish him to join them in the library. Lucy reassured him, "You will talk to Tommy tomorrow, and I am sure he will understand". But she could not reassure him about the library, even though she wished she could.

The next morning while the Alden family was still at home, Rev. Watson called and announced he would stop by in the early afternoon to let them know what had been decided about the library. When he visited, he explained that the library would be closed for a few weeks, except for the first floor where all the classes were being held. In the meantime, the library board would decide if they needed to close a large part of the library for a longer period of time. They would have to review the finances before making any further decisions.

Matthew was not yet home from school, but Lucy knew that this news would worry him further. She arranged with Rev. Watson for Matthew to spend part of that day and the next in the Secret Chambers since he would not be able to go there for the foreseeable future. When Matthew came home, Lucy told him the news. She said that the two of them could go to the Secret Chambers for a few hours after he ate dinner.

The Big Room and the Small Room were not only places where Matthew explored his love of reading. They also connected him to his grandmother. Matthew already missed her since she was not showing up in his dreams anymore. He knew that the closing of the Secret Chambers would only be temporary, and he told himself that he would enjoy it even more after it reopened. Still, he would miss going there while the library was closed.

Renewal of friendship

Matthew and Lucy went to the Secret Chambers that afternoon, and Lucy promised him that Tommy would also come. She had spoken to Clara and arranged for all four of them to meet in the Secret Chambers. Both Tommy and Matthew felt a little embarrassed when they saw each other and were not sure what to say. They both started to speak at the same time.

"I am sorry ...", "I did not know ...". This made them laugh, and then Matthew continued, "I did not know the door was closed and I am sorry you could not come in. It must have been awful to think that we did not want to let you in. I am very sorry you felt that".

Tommy said, "Oh I am sorry and embarrassed at the same time. You could have been in a real danger, but I concluded that I was not welcome. You never gave me any reason to doubt your loyalty, and the closed door should have alerted me that something was amiss. Instead I thought there was a problem in our friendship even though we never had one so far". He looked embarrassed.

"It's okay", said Matthew. Tommy hesitated and then added, "I thought you liked Nika and wanted to spend time only with her. That I was in the way".

A DRY PERIOD

"Oh!" exclaimed Matthew. "I do like Nika, very much, but you were not in the way. And if I ever wanted to spend time with only her or only you, I could just say it." Matthew was still rather innocent; there was nothing malicious in him. He hated to think that his friend thought he was not welcome in his company anymore. After they affirmed that their friendship was as strong and valuable as ever, they were both reminded of the fourth rule from *"Only Children"*. After their recent experience, it proved more relevant. The rule went like this,

Rule Four

My dear child, the fourth rule in keeping your innocence is to check what someone meant before you decide their actions or words are meant to cause hurt and bring discord between you. Sometimes you will misunderstand what other people say or do. It is wise to check first that you understood their intentions before you jump to conclusions and react. It is human to react; human, but not wise. We all react to people from time to time in ways we prefer not to. But if you practice responding to others with understanding and kindness while there is no problem between you, it will be easier to do the same in times when you feel you've been hurt and the pressure rises.

Try to be aware that everyone carries hurts that you are not responsible for and that have nothing to do with you. Yet people will respond to you through those hurts from time to time.

What is more, kindness is not a value out of which everyone operates. Some people will choose to bring discord. That does not mean you contributed to it. This

can teach you to grow in wisdom while keeping your innocence. As for those who are usually kind, make sure you understand why they said or did something before concluding that they meant to be mean. Practicing this rule will require approaching people with humility. It will open doors for you to preserve friendships and relationships that otherwise would be damaged by misunderstandings that breed mistrust. Be wise and kind in your dealings with others.

Matthew and Tommy liked this rule because they felt it has helped them to smooth the misunderstanding that arose between them on that fateful day when the library was on fire. They spoke about the incident often. Strangely, the experience helped them to be more honest in their friendship. They learned that challenges are not always negative; they can help people create a deeper bond when approached with creativity, honesty, and kindness.

A dry period

Matthew missed going to the library, but he occupied himself with schoolwork. Tommy and Nika visited him a few times a week, and sometimes he visited them, but they did not spend as much time together as they did when the Secret Chambers were open. From time to time Matthew asked Rev. Watson if he had any news as to when they would be able to go to the library again, but so far Rev. Watson did not have anything to report.

Matthew was given permission to take two books out of the library before the Secret Chambers were closed. He promised he would look after them. He took *"The Chronicles of Narnia"* from the Big Room and *"Only Children"* from the Small Room. He was rereading the chapters from *"Only Children"* in order to remember them when he grew up. He decided to talk to Lucy and Tom about it.

"Mum? Dad?".

"Yes, honey", said Lucy.

"What is it, Matthew?", Tom added.

"I was thinking about remembering. It is quite important to remember things, isn't it?"

"Which things?", Lucy asked.

"Well, I am thinking of Grandmother", said Matthew. "I never knew her, but the stories about her teach me about our family story. Her letters, the dreams, the book she left for me as a gift, and the Secret Chambers connect me to who she was when she was alive. It is good for me to know that my grandmother loved reading so much that she started a bookstore and then left the books she gathered through the years to the library. She inspires me to love learning and reading. Also, because someone in my family was very generous and we are all affected by it in a good way, I'm encouraged to be generous too."

"Is there something else that made you think about remembering?", said Tom, who had a sense that there was more to it than what Matthew already shared.

"Well, yes", said Matthew. "The book *Only Children* made me think of it. If I do not remember the lessons that are in the book, as an adult when I will not be able to read them, I may forget to apply them. The rules are very useful and wise, and Grandmother must have had a good reason to write them for children."

"What do you think the reason was?", Lucy asked.

"I think it was to prepare us for life", Matthew started to explain when he saw Tom reaching out towards the book. Matthew stood up, went to Tom, and put his hand on the book. He said, "Dad, you cannot read the book. I can tell you what is in it, but I am sorry, you cannot read it". Matthew was adamant. "Grandmother had a reason to write it only for children, and the book was to be stored in the Small Room, where only children can enter." Matthew emphasised the word *children*. "In that room there was no chance of disobeying Grandmother's instructions as no older person would have been able to enter. I do not wish to disrespect Grandmother's wishes, so if you would excuse me, I would be grateful if you do not read it."

Tom loosened his grip on the book and let Matthew have it. "I am sorry, Matthew. I did not wish to upset you. I simply wanted to see what the book was about so that I could understand why it was so important to remember it. When I was a child, this book was not around. But I understand not wanting to disobey Grandmother and her instructions, and so I will not read it. But if you would like to tell me about the rules, I would like to learn about them, and it will help you remember too," said Tom with a wink. Matthew was quite relieved that he did not have to argue about this, and he gladly spoke about the rules, as he remembered them.

After some time, Lucy said, "You started telling us earlier why you thought the rules were written for children. Do you want to tell us more about that now?" She was slightly annoyed at Tom for disrupting Matthew's thought process. She wondered if Matthew would manage to recall what he wanted to say earlier.

A DRY PERIOD

"Well", said Matthew, "I think Grandmother wrote the rules for children because she thought we would be able to understand them. Maybe we are not yet wise and learned like the adults are, and our experiences are limited compared to yours, but some things come naturally to children. It is easier to learn a lesson about something that comes naturally to us, especially when it is explained well and when deep meaning is given to it, than to learn something that is quite unnatural to us. In this second case, no matter how much someone tries to persuade us that something is valuable to learn, we will struggle with it".

Lucy and Tom were amazed at what Matthew was saying. They simply kept listening, without interrupting.

Matthew went on. "For example, Grandmother said some people forget they ever had dreams and they do not know they have the key to unlock some of those dreams again. They can start living from their centre, from the heart. They were always meant to explore those dreams, but they had forgotten it. Maybe they were too afraid to try. If they have forgotten their dreams, it will be harder to remind them, and more painful too, than if they had learned in childhood to hold onto dreams and made sure not to forget them. That is why I was thinking how valuable remembering is. In my case, remembering Grandmother's rules will help prepare me for life. I am too young to know some of those things, even if they come more naturally to me. But reading the instructions from Grandmother and applying what she says will make my life richer now as well as later."

Matthew did not know if anything he said made sense, but Tom and Lucy looked at each other and smiled.

Tom said, "I think we should make these conversations a weekly routine".

"Yes", agreed Lucy. "Matthew, it would help you to practice Grandmother's rules. Besides, as you talk about them and what is important to your young mind and heart, we would learn from these conversations. Veronica had read me chapters in her book as she wrote them, but I had forgotten them."

Tom added, "Yes, we were children once too, and the innocence that was in us then remains stored somewhere inside our hearts. These conversations would be good for all of us, not only for you, Matthew".

They all agreed that these conversations would help the whole family practice Grandmother's rules and grow closer together.

Chapter 5

The New Girl

That same evening before retiring for the night, Lucy and Tom spoke about how proud they were of their boy. Matthew went to sleep happy that he was able to share with his parents what was on his mind. He was grateful that they listened to him. Family conversations became part of the weekly routine, and Lewis would often join in too.

The next day Matthew went to school still thinking of the conversation he had with his parents on the importance of remembering. It was a beautiful morning in early May.

Matthew thought it was going to be a usual day spent attending classes; some he would enjoy, some he would find boring. He knew the homework would be examined and new homework given. He was looking forward to chats with old friends during the breaks and did not expect any particular surprise. But one never knows what a day will bring. If there are surprises in store we can never know if they will be happy, or sad, or a mixture of both.

When Tommy and Nika approached him in the school yard, he nearly failed to notice them. The noise of other children was

VERONICA'S BOOKSTORE

very loud and Matthew was still deep in his thoughts. "Hey, Matthew, there is some exciting news for us today!", exclaimed Nika. It took Matthew a few moments to gather himself and to realise she was talking to him. "Oh, sorry. I was thinking about something." He smiled. "Hi, Tommy and Nika, good to see you. What were you saying?"

They smiled too and then they grabbed his arms and shouted with one voice, "We have news! We have a new girl in our school!". Both of them could hardly contain themselves.

"Why are you so excited, Tommy? You are not in the same class as us. Or are you talking about someone in your class?" Matthew was confused.

Nika jumped in. "No, she is in *our* class, but we can all be friends with her!"

"That sounds good", said Matthew, still confused.

The first class in the morning was geography. As Matthew and Nika entered the classroom, Matthew saw the new girl for the first time. She was a black girl with long, curly, brownish hair. Her brown eyes were bright and big. She was beautiful. Matthew gasped. Never before had his knees felt unstable. Nor had he ever experienced a pain in his stomach that was also sweet. He did not understand this reaction. His eyes were drawn towards her. She was sitting in the third row to his left. Matthew's seat was in the middle of the fourth row. He kept looking in her direction, even though he tried not to make it obvious.

After the class was over, he ran outside. Nika ran after him, but she could not find him. He hid in the toilet until the break was over. He knew Nika would tell him to go and talk to the new girl, and he could not do that. Not with his knees shaking and this pain in the stomach. He would talk to Lucy tonight about this, and then maybe he could speak to the new girl tomorrow. He avoided Nika for the rest of the day, which was not that easy since she kept trying to talk to him. Eventually Nika distracted herself with other things and decided she was going to talk to the new girl after school.

At home

Matthew was home unusually early because as soon as school was over he had left. Lucy was working at home that afternoon and was surprised to see Matthew come in so soon. He looked like he had been running, so Lucy was afraid something bad had happened.

"Weren't you supposed to meet with Tommy after school today?", said Lucy.

"Oh, I forgot", said Matthew. "I will call him and say we can meet another day. I did not see him when I came out of school."

Though Lucy was still concerned, she said calmly, "Is everything all right? You sound like you ran from the school. Did something bad happen?"

Matthew looked embarrassed. "No, not bad. Just unusual. We have a new student in the class. It's a girl. She is really beautiful. I was petrified to talk to her, and I really wanted to. I was shy and did not want anyone to know it, so I ran home after school. So, yes, I did run. Oh, I'm sure that sounds silly." He was defensive.

"It's ok, Matthew", said Lucy. "Do you like this new girl?"

THE NEW GIRL

"How do you mean, like her? I don't even know her!", exclaimed Matthew.

"Well", Lucy replied, "you said she was beautiful. That's what I mean by like. Maybe you are experiencing what it means to be in love. It is uncomfortable at first, especially when it is new. If you have never experienced it before, I presume the experience would scare you."

"Yes, it was scary. And it was enjoyable as well", said Matthew quite confused.

"Did you talk to her?", asked Lucy.

"No!" Matthew did not know why he shouted the answer. "I was afraid to. Maybe tomorrow."

"Do you want to tell me more about it?", Lucy asked. She sat down in the living room, and made a gesture to Matthew to join her.

After a deep sigh he said, "Why was I so afraid to talk to her?"

"Did you think she would not want to talk to you?", suggested Lucy.

"I don't know", said Matthew. "Normally I am not afraid of that. She was so beautiful that I could not think. It's more . . . how she held herself. I mean, she had a beautiful face, too. But it was more than that. She looked confident, which was very attractive and so scary. I thought I would not know what to say, so I avoided her. Actually, I avoided everyone else too."

"Did they notice?", asked Lucy.

"Nika must have", answered Matthew. "She was chasing me for most of the day. It was so exhausting trying to avoid her, and I felt bad about it as well. But I could not tell her the reason why I was not able to talk to the new girl."

"Do you know the new girl's name?"

"No, I don't. I know nothing about her. Only . . .", he did not finish the sentence.

"Only that you like her?", uttered Lucy.

"Yes", said Matthew quietly.

"Don't worry. Let your feelings settle. You can talk to her tomorrow. Is that's something you want to do?"

"Well, yes", was the reply, "but I am not sure I will calm down sufficiently till tomorrow. Can you tell me what to do if the way I feel does not change?"

Lucy and Matthew spoke for another hour, and Matthew found it helpful to be able to put into words how he was feeling and what he was experiencing. Tom and Lewis came in. Tom was making dinner that evening, so he greeted them quickly and went to the kitchen to prepare the meal. Lewis sat at the table and was reading something while Lucy and Matthew continued the conversation. They also spoke about the Secret Chambers and how they both missed going there.

Eventually Lucy asked, "Do you feel a little bit better now? Is there anything else that could help you when you go to school tomorrow?"

THE NEW GIRL

81

"Not that I could think of. I do feel better", said Matthew with a sigh. "It is good to know that strong feelings like that are normal in some situations. Thank you for helping me to be comfortable with being uncomfortable." He said this rather seriously.

Lucy laughed, "I would not put it better myself. You are welcome, my dear. You are welcome".

They had dinner and afterwards Matthew had a sudden idea. He decided to write a letter to the new girl. It was not a letter he meant to send, but after talking to Lucy, he decided he would write down his thoughts in order to sort them out. He did not fully know what he was thinking - his thoughts were a mess - but he hoped writing them was going to help. And it did.

The next day

Matthew was excited the next morning. Talking to Lucy put him at ease, and the night's sleep helped. When he met Nika and Tommy at school he wanted to apologise, but they were both still so engrossed in talking about the new girl that there was no need. Matthew was relieved. However, he still felt apprehensive about meeting her. Her name was Jasmine, he learned from Nika. He was so distracted the day before that he did not notice anyone mention her name. Jasmine was talking to a few children as Matthew and Nika entered the class. Her laughter was vibrant with energy, like a river sparkling in the morning sunshine.

Nika ran towards her and said, "I want you to meet my friend, Matthew!"

Matthew felt a bit more confident than yesterday, but his legs were still somewhat weak and Jasmine's laughter had unlocked something in the middle of his chest. He extended his hand with a beaming smile and said, "Hi, I'm Matthew. Nice to meet you".

Jasmine smiled back, and said, "Hi, Matthew, I heard about you. Nice to meet you too!" They spoke for a few moments, but she soon became distracted with other children greeting her, so Matthew went to his seat pleased with himself. A small achievement perhaps, but he was delighted he did not embarrass himself.

Over the next few weeks, Matthew, Nika and Tommy spent a lot of time with Jasmine. Other children from school joined them as well. Matthew learned to be quite relaxed in Jasmine's company, for which he was very grateful. But he was worried that other children would start asking about his close friendship with Nika and Tommy. *"If they become too inquisitive, they may somehow find out about the Secret Chambers"*, Matthew thought. So far no one knew or asked about it, but he was afraid they would. The part of the library where the Secret Chambers were situated was still closed. He missed going there. Yet he was not ready to speak more publicly about the gift his grandmother left him, whether he could go there or not.

A surprising turn of events

One day after school Matthew, Tommy and Jasmine were supposed to go to a café that was half way between the school and the library on the way to Matthew's house. Nika couldn't join them. Looking pensive and distant, she had told Matthew that she needed to go home after school to help her parents because her dad's mother, who was not well, was visiting. He understood that Nika was worried about her grandmother.

When Matthew came to school that morning, Jasmine was not there and neither was Tommy. He was concerned about his two friends and wondered what happened to them. During the break he was lost in thought when Nika approached him with tears in her eyes. "Someone attacked Jasmine last night", she uttered.

"What do you mean?", asked Matthew, stunned.

"She is fine, but scared, and won't be in school for a few days. Maybe longer", Nika said.

"What happened? Who did it?" Matthew could hardly speak. He felt dizzy and confused.

"I don't know, but someone had a knife and threatened her. There were adults passing by … I think the person with the knife was a boy. The adults stopped him and Jasmine ran home. Her mother called my mother. My mother said both Jasmine and her mother were very upset. Why would someone do that?"

"I was going to ask you the same. Why would someone do that!?"

Both children were in shock. When the break was over and the class resumed, Matthew was in a daze for the rest of the school day. He wanted to ask to be allowed to go home early. He did not feel well, but he did not know how to explain why. He found it odd that teachers said nothing. Possibly they did, but he missed it because he found it very hard to concentrate.

This was the second time Matthew wanted to run home, but today he decided to wait on Nika and walk her home. She was even more distraught than he was. Nika cried as they walked, but they did not speak much. After they parted, Matthew thought it was useless to go to the café now since Jasmine and Tommy wouldn't be there. He still wondered what happened to Tommy. Matthew needed to talk to Lucy or Tom, so he went straight home.

Distressing conversation

When Matthew came home, Tom was waiting for him with a warm meal. "How was your day, young man?"

"Not good, Dad. Quite upsetting actually", answered Matthew.

Tom frowned and invited Matthew to sit down at the table and tell him all about it. Matthew ate slowly as he told Tom what he learned from Nika. "I only know that Jasmine was attacked. I don't know why, and I don't understand. Our town is peaceful." He was looking for reassurance.

"Our town has been peaceful, but there are people who are hostile everywhere. What you described sounds like it could have been a racist attack", said Tom. Matthew has never heard of that word, so Tom explained what it meant.

"Jasmine was attacked because of the colour of her skin?!" Matthew exclaimed loudly. "If they knew her, they would not…", his voice suddenly dropped and terror came over his face.

"What is it Matthew? Did you remember something else?"

"Tommy was not in school either", exclaimed Matthew. "Ok", said Tom.

Matthew continued, "I hope he did not …", but he was not able to finish his sentence.

"I see. I doubt it, son. Will I call his parents to see how he is doing and why he was not at school? I will do that and you finish the food."

"Ok, Dad. I hope it was not him", said Matthew with a sigh. Tom went to another room, spoke on the phone for a few minutes, and then came back to the kitchen.

"Good news, boy. Well, not exactly good, but certainly not as bad as you thought. Tommy had a bug last night and did not feel better this morning, so he stayed in. I told his parents about Jasmine, and they will tell him later when he has recovered a little bit more. It was not Tommy who attacked Jasmine. Is there a reason you thought it might have been?"

"No, Dad. I had no reason. I am just confused. Tommy is not violent and he was delighted, same as everyone, when Jasmine came to our school. Hearing that Jasmine was most likely attacked because of the colour of her skin makes me question everything I know. I never knew people get attacked because they are black. I think that's horrible. I thought it weird that Tommy was not in school as well, so I connected the two . . . but wrongly. That is something Grandmother wrote about not doing. Always check for the truth before you make an assumption."

They moved to the sitting room, still talking. Lucy was teaching in the library, so she came home later. Lewis had a get-together with his old friends, so he came late too. Matthew and Tom talked until Matthew was calm enough to do his homework. Usually he would do it in his room upstairs, but Tom told him he could do it in the sitting room if Tom's company helped him. Lucy found them there, Matthew deep in his geography lesson and Tom reading a book. She had heard what had happened and was concerned about Matthew.

Lucy greeted them both with a smile. Tom got up to talk to her and they embraced. Lucy was grateful that Tom has already spoken with Matthew. Tom then returned to the sitting room and resumed reading his book. Lucy walked over to see how Matthew was getting on with his homework. He was almost finished and tired. Lucy stayed with him until he was done and while he got into bed.

The principal visits the classroom

Next morning Tom suggested to Matthew that he stay at home if he was still distressed from the day before, but Matthew wanted to go to school. There he met Nika. Tommy was back as well, but Jasmine did not appear. Nika had said that Jasmine wouldn't come, so it was not a surprise. The class looked empty without her to Matthew.

Early in the morning their teacher announced that the third class of the day would be a meeting about housekeeping matters. The principal was supposed to join them, too. Everyone Matthew spoke with was in shock and no one was hiding it. During the third class the principal said that Jasmine might not be coming back. Her parents had not decided yet, but they wanted to make sure that Jasmine felt comfortable and would be safe. Matthew had to hold back the tears.

The principal reassured the children that the school was a very positive experience for Jasmine. "She found good friends here and you were very welcoming to her. She wants to thank you all for that. The person who attacked her was not from the school, but the attack has made Jasmine feel unsafe. If any of you need to talk to someone, we have asked Mrs. Avery, our counsellor, to be available throughout the whole week. Either approach Mrs. Avery directly or talk to your teacher and she will put you in touch with her. Also, I want to stress that we condemn any attack on any of our students, no matter what their colour or religious background. We are here to support you. If you need anything or have questions, please let us know."

A number of students availed of the counselling the school offered. Matthew, Nika, and Tommy wondered if they would ever see Jasmine again. Missing her made them sad, but it drew them closer.

News about the Secret Chambers

One Saturday morning when Matthew was still asleep, Rev. Watson came to the house. He had good news about the reopening of the library. Lucy and Tom were delighted to hear that Matthew would soon be allowed to visit the Secret Chambers again. Some of the library would remain closed to the public for now, but most of the funding was secured and there was no danger of any part of the library closing permanently. Lucy and Tom breathed a sigh of relief.

"I am glad we have good news to tell Matthew. The children are still distressed with what happened to Jasmine", said Lucy. "I think Jasmine is still in town. Perhaps the children can take her to the Secret Chambers and give her something nice to remember — if her parents will agree, of course".

When Matthew woke up, he was delighted to hear about the Secret Chambers. His face glowed when Lucy told him that soon he could visit the Big Room and the Small Room again. He ran into her embrace. They laughed. "I missed going there, Mum."

"I know, dear. I did too, I have to admit." Lucy told him about her idea of bringing Jasmine there, which made Matthew even more enthusiastic.

"We can make sure she has a good experience!", said Matthew. "Maybe that will help erase the bad!"

Lucy smiled and said, "It won't erase it, darling, but it may help her for sure. I will see what her parents think of the idea. It would be good to invite Jasmine's mother, too, so that she does not feel worried about where Jasmine is going. While it is good that the Chambers are not public, so Jasmine can relax, we do call it the *Secret* Chambers. When you have a bad experience like Jasmine had, secrets can scare you. Hopefully she and her mother will be open to coming, but don't get too excited just yet", warned Lucy.

Meeting Jasmine again

Jasmine's mum, Lisa, was very grateful to hear from Lucy. She was touched at the offer Lucy suggested, but she was not sure if it was a good idea. Jasmine was still rather afraid after the incident. She was not comfortable in public places. "I will talk to Jasmine and let you know", Lisa said. Later that same afternoon, she called Lucy. "I was wrong, Jasmine would love to join you. I will come, too, if that is still okay with you. I need a break from reality myself. It will be nice to do something a bit different. And sharing a good experience with Jasmine will give us something else to talk about. I think I will be able to support her better if I join you."

Lucy spoke with Rev. Watson, and they arranged for a Saturday afternoon two weeks later. Matthew was very excited. Nika and Tommy were coming as well, and they would see Jasmine for the first time after her horrible experience. Her parents were keeping her home from school until then.

Matthew has not had a dream about his grandmother in a long time. He did not expect to have one again, especially not very soon. But the night before going back to the Secret Chambers, he dreamed about Veronica.

"Don't forget to practice the rules of keeping your childhood innocence, child. There will come a time, and it could be soon, when innocence won't be so natural to you, if you don't practice it."

These words are all that Matthew remembered from the dream. The rest of it was in a haze. No matter how much he tried to recall it, he could not remember what the rest of the dream was about. *"Don't forget to practice the rules of keeping your childhood inno*cence . . .", Matthew kept repeating this over and over in his mind. He has not been reading *"Only Children"* ever since Jasmine joined their class. He was too distracted to read anything. But after the dream he decided he would start reading again. *"After all, reading is one of the rules!",* he thought. That morning when he woke up, he packed that book to take back to the Secret Chambers and to the Small Room, where it belonged. He wanted to show it to his friends, Jasmine in particular.

Reunion

It was mid-June. Not even a month had passed since Jasmine's attack. Since then, her parents decided to homeschool Jasmine for now. The library closed for public at two o'clock that afternoon. The private gathering in the Secret Chambers was scheduled for three o'clock. Matthew, Lucy, Tom, and Lewis arrived a little early. Tommy and Nika were next to arrive. Jasmine and her mum came last. They arrived in a car that stopped in front of the library. Lewis escorted them from the entrance of the building to the Big Room. When the three of them appeared there, the children were very excited to see Jasmine. They all ran towards her and she ran towards them. All of them embraced. There were tears and laughter. This day was like a homecoming to them.

The children were so lost in play that it seemed like the time stopped. For most of it they did not think of anything distressing, though at the start they did want to know how Jasmine was. They listened as she described the night a child she never met threatened her on the street. "I am still scared. My parents told me it will take time. But being here with all of you helps. I missed you", she said with a smile. "Knowing that I have good friends helps me to forget that bad experience ... for a moment, anyway."

Later on Matthew showed them "*Only Children*" in the Small Room. The room was too small for all four of them, so they took turns in going inside. They each took time to read the book for a while. They also spoke about Veronica and most of all, they laughed.

Lucy, Tom, Lewis, and Lisa enjoyed hearing their laughter. Even the adults started to laugh, as if something was healed within them. Lisa was deeply moved with the gathering. As they parted in the evening, they decided to meet like this again. Matthew was very happy when he and his family arrived home. But he was also tired. Lucy and Tom had another piece of news for him. They decided to tell him in the morning.

Chapter 6

The Old Bookstore

Matthew again started going to the Secret Chambers a few times a week. Sometimes he would go on his own to read; other times Tommy, Nika or Jasmine would join him. One day Matthew was there with Lewis. While Lewis occupied himself by reading the newspapers, Matthew took time to explore. He walked through the corridor that had shelves with books on each side and led to the Big Room. He looked over the titles, the covers, large and smaller books, until somewhere in the middle a book grabbed his attention. He ran his fingers along its edges and pulled it out.

The book had dark-red covers, almost brown. It looked old, but well preserved. He opened the book and noticed a stamp from the old bookstore on the opening page. "Veronica's Bookstore", it said. Matthew gasped. He opened a few books surrounding that one. They all were stamped the same but had different years of publication. He saw 1938, 1921, 1946, 1967, and one as old as 1892. All the years seemed so exotic to him, distant and mysterious. The book with dark-red covers in particular stirred his curiosity about the old bookstore. As he glanced at it, he saw that Veronica Stone was its author.

On the way home Matthew spoke to Lewis about what he saw. "Yes, the books in that section are all marked with the stamp from the bookstore. That's right", said Lewis. "Those were some of Veronica's favourite books. We still have the stamp in the shop. I have not been there in months. The dust must look dreadful! If you wanted to, we could go and explore one day, and I could show you the old stamps." Matthew was delighted with that idea.

The bookstore was in the upper town, ten minutes away from Matthew's family house. The upper town or the old town, as they called it, was rather small. Only a few cobbled stone streets ran under the old street lamps. The bookstore sat on a narrow street off the Main Street. With all the happenings of the last months, no one from Matthew's family has been to it in a long time.

The old bookstore

Veronica's Bookstore was closed for years, but it still had a good selection of books. Lewis and Matthew went there one Saturday afternoon in late June. The last time they went there together was in winter. Lewis had handed Matthew the key to the bookstore. He now had it in his pocket and was squeezing it as they walked. At first he could not tell the reason for doing it. Then it dawned on him; the key reminded him of the key of forgotten dreams that Veronica left in her book "*Only Children*". This key was simply bigger; otherwise the resemblance was quite striking.

Matthew thought, "*The bookstore is somehow forgotten by all of us since we discovered the Secret Chambers. Could it be that the bookstore is a forgotten dream?*" As soon as they approached the door to Veronica's Bookstore, Matthew forgot that thought as if it dropped on the sideway and fell into the cracks among the cobbled stones.

Inside, the bookstore was a mess. Books were piled up on the table in the middle of the room, some were on the chair. One could guess where they belonged because there were empty spaces on the shelves that stretched all along the wall. "Be careful where you walk, Matthew", said Lewis. "I started sorting the books into the boxes since the last time we were here. As you can see, there are lots of boxes on the floor. I did not finish. I miss Veronica dreadfully when I am here, so after a while I find it too hard to keep coming back. There are so many memories attached to this place."

"Granddad, let's go upstairs, and you can tell me some of those stories", said Matthew.

Sturdy wooden stairs in the far corner of the shop led upstairs to what used to be the office. Veronica preferred to call it "the sorting place". Drawers kept a record of all the books she ever had in the shop and the number of copies sold. There were three sofas upstairs with tall lamps next to them. Matthew and Lewis removed the dust from two of them, turned on the lamps, and sat to talk. The lamps gave a warm glow.

"This is where I met Veronica, in this shop. We were both young. I still remember that she was wearing a red linen dress. I was afraid of her self-assuredness. I did not think she would like me. She was always friendly, but I was conflicted with too many things. She wasn't. I started helping in the bookstore one day a week. One of those days she told me to go pick something up upstairs. There were several people in the shop, and it was quite noisy. She came upstairs a minute after me. She startled me. Looking me straight in the eyes she said, "A man is not a man until he knows how to love". Then she went back downstairs. I am still puzzled by that sometimes. I think she only told me to go upstairs because that's where it was quieter. She could not

THE OLD BOOKSTORE

tell me that personal statement downstairs, with all the people around.

After that day I got courage to ask her out. Ever since I can remember, I have had inner conflict with myself. I have tried to hide it, and I think I did it well. Veronica loved me through it, not expecting me to change. I learned to relax over the years. She taught me so much."

Seeing tears in Lewis's eyes, Matthew got up, put his hand on his granddad's shoulder and said, "Granddad, she is still around. I know it's not the same. I never knew you miss her that much. But maybe...", Matthew hesitated.

"Maybe?", asked Lewis.

Matthew continued, "Well, maybe we can reopen Veronica's Bookstore. It has been closed for very long. Perhaps you never finished packing the books because you were not meant to. This was Grandmother's dream, this shop. Maybe we can open it again, if it won't be too hard for you to be here regularly".

Matthew did not fully understand the reason for saying all this. He again thought of the key of forgotten dreams. "We can make new memories", added Matthew.

Lewis's face brightened. "Let me think about it, my boy. I will talk to your parents and then we can decide. It is not a bad idea, Matthew. Not a bad idea at all", said Lewis, as he got up. "Let me show you the stamps that got your attention in the library."

Lewis went to a drawer at the far end of the room, opened it and took out the stamps for marking the books. The stamps looked old. Matthew took one, touched the bottom that leaves the mark, and said, "It would be good to use these again".

The news

When they got home that evening, Lucy and Tom were laughing in the sitting room. Lewis and Matthew joined them. Matthew did not manage to say much about their day before Lucy said, "Sit here, Matthew. We have something to tell you". Lucy seemed quite cheerful. Matthew felt a little apprehensive because he found that even good news can be rather overwhelming. This showed on his face.

"No need to be afraid", Lucy said as she put her hand on Matthew's arm. "We have been wanting to tell you for some time. We are having a baby. In six months you will have a brother or a sister. You used to tell me when you were younger how you always wanted one. What do you say?" She waited for Matthew's reaction. His face lit up.

"Oh, a brother or a sister! Can I have both?!"

They all laughed.

"I think this time it will be only one", said Lucy.

Excitedly Matthew said, "I will be able to show them the Secret Chambers! I mean, him or her". But then his face dropped. He looked concerned.

"What is it, son?", asked Tom.

"Well, it means that we won't be able to open the bookstore again if you will have to look after a small baby."

"Open the bookstore again!", exclaimed Lucy and Tom at the same time. They looked at Lewis, who burst into the heartiest laughter. He said, "We spent the afternoon in the bookstore, as you know, and afterwards I told Matthew some of the stories about Veronica . . ." He stopped. "Actually, I admitted I missed her. Because I do, very much. Matthew had the idea of opening the bookstore again. I told him we would talk to the two of you before we decide. But I kind of like the idea." Lewis smiled.

Matthew looked at Lucy and Tom and then said, "The key to Veronica's Bookstore reminded me of the key that Grandmother left in that book *"Only Children"*. It was the key of forgotten dreams. I think they are the same key, just a different size! They look so alike. Grandmother loved the bookstore. I know she left us the Secret Chambers, which I really love, but it would be a terrible pity if her bookstore ended up a ruin. I would like to bring her dream back to life".

Lucy sighed. "That is a big decision to make", she said, "but perhaps it could be done. Let's leave it for now. We can talk about it over the next few days and see what to do about it." What she did not tell them is that she had had another dream about Veronica. She would not have called it 'prophetic', but after the conversation they just had, this word was roaming around her mind.

The dream

Lucy got used to having dreams about her mother. But they were usually about the past or about things happening at present. The dream from the previous night was unusual. It was the only dream Lucy had that was about the future.

In the dream Lucy entered a newly refurbished shop. It resembled her mother's bookstore, but there was something modern about it. She saw a new desk, where her mother used to sit. The stairs at the back also looked new. The bookshelves were sturdy and same beautiful mahogany colour as the stairs. Books were sorted by subjects, with each section in alphabetical order. All of a sudden she saw her mother sitting at the desk, smiling, like she used to.

"What do you think, Lucy?", said Veronica.

"It looks amazing", answered Lucy. "It reminds me of the time you looked after it, only it's more modern."

"It has the most recent titles. You also made some improvements in managing the business", added Veronica. "New generations always bring something fresh. This is how it will look when Matthew takes over, and later when his sister joins him." Veronica was revealing facts about the future that she already knew.

When Lucy woke up, she put the hands on her belly and thought, *"I don't know if I am carrying a girl or a boy. How would Veronica know?"* The dream puzzled her. Throughout the day she drifted into her thoughts more than once.

Tom noticed but did not say anything until later in the day. "What is it, honey? Where have you gone this time?", Tom smiled as if teasing her.

"I had a dream. I know that a lot of my dreams seem strange to you. This one was the most unusual, and it confused me", said Lucy. "I promise to tell you about it in the evening, when Matthew goes to sleep. I prefer to get my mind off it until then, and you can help distract me by discussing our baby's room", said Lucy with a twinkle in her eye.

As they talked about the room they must prepare for the new child, they were overjoyed. That is why Matthew and Lewis heard them laughing when they got back from the bookstore.

Decision

Over the next few days Lucy and Tom spoke about the possibility of reopening the bookstore. Lewis was cheerful. Talking about making Veronica's dream a reality again reenergised him. Matthew was determined. He saw no obstacles. Perhaps that is what Grandmother meant about childhood innocence; he had not yet learned that reality can discourage people from dreaming. Finally the family decided to go ahead and reopen the bookstore.

Work began in earnest. Together with Lewis, Matthew found people who could help them build new bookshelves. Rev. Watson gave him a list of popular titles and best way to get them for Veronica' Bookstore. One day an advertisement appeared in the local newspapers about a grant for an innovative project that would enrich their town.

The whole family worked on filling in the application for the grant, and Lucy then sent it in. Only two projects applied, theirs and one about a short tour visiting the most important sights in the town. The Council realised that the two projects would feed into each other and promote their town simultaneously. They decided to sponsor both.

Veronica was very much loved in the town. Everyone had been sad when Veronica's Bookstore closed, so the idea of reopening was welcomed. People offered to help make it a reality.

"This is happening too easily", said Lucy rather surprised.

"As if your mother is behind it", concluded Tom through laughter. Lucy smiled, not really knowing what to say to that.

Everything did go very smoothly. It only took three months for improvements to be made in the shop. They started planning in early July, the beginning of the summer holidays for Matthew. The new books started to arrive that month. During the next two months the furniture was bought, the door was repainted, and the sign at the entrance was made to look like new. The most tedious part was cataloging and deciding the price for each book. This was left until the end. Three months after they first spoke about reopening, Veronica's Bookstore was ready.

Reopening

The family decided to open Veronica's Bookstore on the first Monday in October that year. The notice announcing it was put in the local newspaper, and posters were displayed on a few significant buildings in town. Other than that, they did not make huge fuss about the reopening. Lucy was almost seven months pregnant, so they hired a shop assistant.

Lucy and Matthew were both there the first morning. He was allowed to skip school that day. At first a few people came, but then the afternoon brought a bigger number. These visitors were more interested in the story about the bookstore than in the books.

Rev. Watson organised refreshments for reopening, and the library staff helped with serving drinks on the day. Rev. Watson was delighted to see the bookstore open again. The older visitors had known Veronica. One of them was Geraldine, an elderly lady who had been a bit younger than Veronica. She came in with her daughter and was using a walker, so she could not move fast.

THE OLD BOOKSTORE

101

As Geraldine recalled the time when the old bookstore was in town, with Veronica still around, she had tears in her eyes. She said, "Today it is as if part of my childhood has returned". She laughed. "It feels awfully odd to say that. I'm one of the oldest people in town." Her eyes were shining with excitement.

There were more people like her, each bringing their own story about Veronica. Children had heard so much about the bookstore from their parents and grandparents that they were enchanted even before entering. The story of Veronica's Bookstore was like a fairytale to them, and it was even more alluring because this one was a real story that they could walk into today. Children as small as three or four stood next to a bookshelf as if mesmerised.

Lucy approached one little boy. "Hi! Is there a certain book you like?"

"Hi!", he replied. "No, I just like the look of them all. Did Ms Veronica really live here before?" Lucy laughed. "She worked here, yes. But she lived in another house. Did you hear much about her?"

The child continued, "I heard stories about how this bookstore began and I always liked the sound of it. It must have been wonderful to be a child at that time. You brought that magic to us now. Thank you!" The child cried as he grabbed Lucy's leg and held her tightly. Lucy was deeply moved by this gesture. She gently unloosened the boy and called his mother.

All that week people were coming to the bookstore. Some bought books, or at least were interested in exploring which books were on offer. Most, however, merely came to see the new bookstore, to hear the story of its past and to be a part of this great story that they associated with Veronica.

The family was excited about the bookstore. Due to her pregnancy, Lucy was not working anymore, so she would go to the bookstore for a few hours each day. Every evening, Matthew, Lucy, Tom and Lewis sat around the kitchen table to discuss how the day had gone.

At least twice a week Matthew still went to the Secret Chambers. Lewis or Tom took him. Sometimes Tommy, Nika, and Jasmine would join him there. Matthew's friends also visited Veronica'a Bookstore. They enjoyed hearing stories about the old bookstore and what it looked like in Veronica's time.

"I love how Matthew brought his grandmother's dream back to life", said Tommy. Nika and Jasmine agreed.

And yet the Secret Chambers appealed more to Matthew's friends. It was their secret haven that ignited their imagination and helped them to nurture friendship. There were also plenty of books to read, and since Matthew decided not to open the Secret Chambers to the public, they could read, play and talk without being interrupted.

At the end of the first week of reopening the bookstore, the whole family escorted Matthew to the library. As they were sitting in the Big Room, Lewis joked, "I am not surprised people are more into Veronica, than into books. I absolutely share their sentiment".

Matthew was a bit more serious about the whole thing. "Grandmother brought the love of books into town. She encouraged people to read. I am sure we will do the same. And it is amazing that the greatest story they will hear is actually about Grandmother. I could never imagine how exciting and challenging this year was going to turn out to be. I have heard

THE OLD BOOKSTORE

people say, "Be careful what you wish for". I would rather say, "If you wish for something, expect more than you wish for!"

Matthew smiled as he looked at Lucy. He continued, "I wanted to get to know Grandmother, but I got more than stories about Grandmother. She inspired me not to forget good things, not to forget dreams, her own dreams too. It is so good that the bookstore is working again. I hope we can inspire others to find their dreams. Maybe Veronica's Bookstore is not about books at all", said Matthew, not quite sure why he was saying it.

Lucy, Tom and Lewis all smiled.

Maybe indeed the bookstore was not only about books, but about life and stories and dreams, all of which can be found in the best of books. Yet each human heart has stories and dreams too. And sometimes we need a child to remind us of things that truly matter.

Iva Beranek

Iva Beranek is a writer, a speaker and a spiritual director. She was born in Croatia, where her family inspired her love of storytelling. As a teenager, Iva had a great desire to move to Ireland, but she had to wait a number of years for this dream to be fulfilled. Now she lives in Dublin, Ireland, where she completed a doctoral degree in Christian Spirituality.

Iva is a seasoned contributor to "A Living Word" (RTÉ Radio 1) and she presented one of her short stories for "Sunday Miscellany" (RTÉ Radio 1). Iva is a published poet, and she published numerous articles on Christian spirituality. Iva has an immense love for the beauty of nature and of wildlife, and when urban foxes found a home in her garden, she experienced a harmony with them which was reminiscent of the harmony in the garden of Eden.

Her Catholic faith is very important to her, and even though she was not raised in a Catholic family as a child, she believes that God is very close to children.

You can contact Iva and follow her on Instagram @ivadublin.

Printed in Great Britain
by Amazon